THE PENGUIN POETS

CEMETERY NIGHTS

Stephen Dobyns's first volume of poetry, *Concurring Beasts*, won the Lamont Prize. His fifth, *Black Dog, Red Dog*, was a National Poetry Series selection for 1984. He is the author of seven novels, including *Dancer with One Leg*, *Cold Dog Soup*, and four crime novels set in Saratoga Springs, New York. Mr. Dobyns currently lives in Newton, Massachusetts.

POETRY

CEMETERY NIGHTS (1987)
BLACK DOG, RED DOG (1984)
THE BALTHUS POEMS (1982)
HEAT DEATH (1980)
GRIFFON (1976)
CONCURRING BEASTS (1972)

NOVELS

SARATOGA SNAPPER (1986)
COLD DOG SOUP (1985)
SARATOGA HEADHUNTER (1985)
DANCER WITH ONE LEG (1983)
SARATOGA SWIMMER (1981)
SARATOGA LONGSHOT (1976)
A MAN OF LITTLE EVILS (1973)

CEMETERY NIGHTS

POEMS BY
STEPHEN DOBYNS

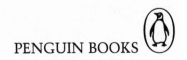
PENGUIN BOOKS

PENGUIN BOOKS
Viking Penguin Inc., 40 West 23rd Street,
New York, New York 10010, U.S.A.
Penguin Books Ltd, Harmondsworth,
Middlesex, England
Penguin Books Australia Ltd, Ringwood,
Victoria, Australia
Penguin Books Canada Limited, 2801 John Street,
Markham, Ontario, Canada L3R 1B4
Penguin Books (N.Z.) Ltd, 182–190 Wairau Road,
Auckland 10, New Zealand

First published in 1987 by Viking Penguin Inc. in
simultaneous hardcover and paperback editions
Published simultaneously in Canada

LIBRARY OF CONGRESS CATALOGING IN PUBLICATION DATA
Dobyns, Stephen, 1941–
Cemetery nights.
I. Title.
PS3554.02C4   1987b   811'.54   86-20501
ISBN 0 14 058.584 2

Printed in the United States of America by
R. R. Donnelley & Sons Company, Harrisonburg, Virginia
Set in Trump Mediæval
Designed by Ginger Legato

For Ellen Bryant Voigt

The wandering earth herself may be
Only a sudden flaming word,
In clanging space a moment heard,
Troubling the endless reverie.
                              —W. B. Yeats

Loss is change and change is Nature's delight. This has
been true from the beginning and will be true till the
end. Then how can you say it is wrong, forever wrong,
that no power in heaven can fix it, and that the world
lies condemned to a thralldom of ills unrelenting?
                              —Marcus Aurelius

We're going boom, boom, boom—
that's the way we live.
                  —Talking Heads

CONTENTS

CEMETERY NIGHTS

CEMETERY NIGHTS

Sweet dreams, sweet memories, sweet taste of earth:
here's how the dead pretend they're still alive—
one drags up a chair, a lamp, unwraps
the newspaper from somebody's garbage,
then sits holding the paper up to his face.
No matter if the lamp is busted and his eyes
have fallen out. Or some of the others
group together in front of the TV, chuckling
and slapping what's left of their knees.
No matter if the screen is dark. Four more
sit at a table with glasses and plates,
lift forks to their mouths and chew. No matter
if their plates are empty and they chew only air.
Two of the dead roll on the ground,
banging and rubbing their bodies together
as if in love or frenzy. No matter if their skin
breaks off, that their genitals are just a memory.

The head cemetery rat calls in all the city rats,
who pay him what rats find valuable—
the wing of a pigeon or ear of a dog.
The rats perch on tombstones and the cheap
statues of angels and, oh, they hold their bellies
and laugh, laugh until their guts half break;
while the stars give off the same cold light
that all these dead once planned their lives by,
and in someone's yard a dog barks and barks
just to see if some animal as dumb as he is
will wake from sleep and perhaps bark back.

THE GARDENER

After the first astronauts reached heaven
the only god discovered in residence
retired to a little brick cottage
in the vicinity of Venus. He was not
unduly surprised. He had seen it coming
since Luther. Besides, what with the imminence
of nuclear war, his job was nearly over.
As soon as the fantastic had become
a commonplace, bus tours were organized,
and once or twice a day the old fellow
would be trotted out from his reading of Dante
and asked to do a few tricks—lightning bolts,
water spouting from a rock, blood from a turnip.
A few of the remaining cherubim
would fly in figure eights and afterward
sell apples from the famous orchard.
In the evening, the retired god would sometimes
receive a visit from his old friend the Devil.
They would smoke their pipes before the fire.
The Devil would stroke his whiskers and cover
his paws with his long furry tail. The mistake,
he was fond of saying, was to make them in
your image instead of mine. Possibly, said
the ex-deity. He hated arguing. The mistake,
he had often thought, was to experiment
with animal life in the first place when
his particular talent was as a gardener.
How pleasant Eden had been in those early days
with its neat rows of cabbages and beets,
flowering quince, a hundred varieties of rose.
But of course he had needed insects, and then
he made the birds, the red ones which he loved;
later came his experiments with smaller mammals—
squirrels and moles, a rabbit or two. When
the temptation had struck him to make something

really big, he had first conceived of it
as a kind of scarecrow to stand in the middle
of the garden and frighten off predators. What
voice had he listened to that convinced him
to give the creature his own face? No voice
but his own. It had amused him to make
a kind of living mirror, a little homunculus
that could learn a few of his lesser tricks.
And he had imagined sitting in the evening
with his friend the Devil watching the small
human creatures frolic in the grass. They would
be like children, good-natured and always singing.
When had he realized his mistake? Perhaps
when he smiled down at the first and it
didn't smile back; when he reached down to help
it to its feet and it shrugged his hand aside.
Standing up, it hadn't walked on the paths marked
with white stones but on the flowers themselves.
It's lonely, God had said. So he made it a mate,
then watched them feed on each other's bodies,
bicker and fight and trample through his garden,
dissatisfied with everything and wanting to escape.
Naturally, he hadn't objected. Kicked out,
kicked out, who had spread such lies? Shaking
and banging the bars of the great gate, they had
begged him for the chance to make it on their own.

TOMATOES

A woman travels to Brazil for plastic
surgery and a face-lift. She is sixty
and has the usual desire to stay pretty.
Once she is healed, she takes her new face
out on the streets of Rio. A young man
with a gun wants her money. Bang, she's dead.
The body is shipped back to New York,
but in the morgue there is a mix-up. The son
is sent for. He is told that his mother
is one of these ten different women.
Each has been shot. Such is modern life.
He studies them all but can't find her.
With her new face, she has become a stranger.
Maybe it's this one, maybe it's that one.
He looks at their breasts. Which ones nursed him?
He presses their hands to his cheek.
Which ones consoled him? He even tries
climbing into their laps to see which
feels most familiar but the coroner stops him.
Well, says the coroner, which is your mother?
They all are, says the young man, let me
take them as a package. The coroner hesitates,
then agrees. Actually, it solved a lot of problems.
The young man has the ten women shipped home,
then cremates them all together. You've seen
how some people have a little urn on the mantel?
This man has a huge silver garbage can.
In the spring, he drags the garbage can
out to the garden and begins working the teeth,
the ash, the bits of bone into the soil.
Then he plants tomatoes. His mother loved tomatoes.
They grow straight from seed, so fast and big
that the young man is amazed. He takes the first
ten into the kitchen. In their roundness,
he sees his mother's breasts. In their smoothness,

he finds the consoling touch of her hands.
Mother, mother, he cries, and he flings himself
on the tomatoes. Forget about the knife, the fork,
the pinch of salt. Try to imagine the filial
starvation, think of his ravenous kisses.

HOW TO LIKE IT

These are the first days of fall. The wind
at evening smells of roads still to be traveled,
while the sound of leaves blowing across the lawns
is like an unsettled feeling in the blood,
the desire to get in a car and just keep driving.
A man and a dog descend their front steps.
The dog says, Let's go downtown and get crazy drunk.
Let's tip over all the trash cans we can find.
This is how dogs deal with the prospect of change.
But in his sense of the season, the man is struck
by the oppressiveness of his past, how his memories
which were shifting and fluid have grown more solid
until it seems he can see remembered faces
caught up among the dark places in the trees.
The dog says, Let's pick up some girls and just
rip off their clothes. Let's dig holes everywhere.
Above his house, the man notices wisps of cloud
crossing the face of the moon. Like in a movie,
he says to himself, a movie about a person
leaving on a journey. He looks down the street
to the hills outside of town and finds the cut
where the road heads north. He thinks of driving
on that road and the dusty smell of the car
heater, which hasn't been used since last winter.
The dog says, Let's go down to the diner and sniff
people's legs. Let's stuff ourselves on burgers.
In the man's mind, the road is empty and dark.
Pine trees press down to the edge of the shoulder,
where the eyes of animals, fixed in his headlights,
shine like small cautions against the night.
Sometimes a passing truck makes his whole car shake.
The dog says, Let's go to sleep. Let's lie down
by the fire and put our tails over our noses.
But the man wants to drive all night, crossing
one state line after another, and never stop

until the sun creeps into his rearview mirror.
Then he'll pull over and rest awhile before
starting again, and at dusk he'll crest a hill
and there, filling a valley, will be the lights
of a city entirely new to him.
But the dog says, Let's just go back inside.
Let's not do anything tonight. So they
walk back up the sidewalk to the front steps.
How is it possible to want so many things
and still want nothing? The man wants to sleep
and wants to hit his head again and again
against a wall. Why is it all so difficult?
But the dog says, Let's go make a sandwich.
Let's make the tallest sandwich anyone's ever seen.
And that's what they do and that's where the man's
wife finds him, staring into the refrigerator
as if into the place where the answers are kept—
the ones telling why you get up in the morning
and how it is possible to sleep at night,
answers to what comes next and how to like it.

FREAK

For Byron Burford

A child is born with a third eye smack
in the middle of his forehead. It's not
worth much. He can't see with it, can't
ogle with it, he can only blink with it.
But this is good enough to get him a place
in a freak show, so he spends his youth
sitting in a chair blinking his third eye
while crowds of people fall back and gasp.
At first, he doesn't mind being an oddity,
but by the time he is thirty he's grown tired
of traveling and broods about the small town
where he grew up and how he'd like to have a farm.
Therefore, he takes the big step of having
his third eye surgically removed and returns
home and buys a piece of land. But right
from the start it's a mistake—the bank
cheats him on the mortgage, the tractor
salesman sells him a clunker of a tractor,
the hardware cheats him on the price of nails.
But even worse, he's gone from being an ugly
man with a third eye to being plain ugly—
the jerk that the world pokes in the back.
So he sells the farm and returns to the show.
Who wants to be invisible? Billing himself
as the man with the third eye and dressed
in his old spangled tights, he again sits
in a straight chair before people foolish
enough to spend a quarter to see some character
with a badly painted blue eye on his forehead.
What do you see? shouts a joker at the barrier.
But the man is too proud to answer.
He now understands the divisions of the world
and has made his choice, and even a third eye
done with paint is better than no third eye at all.
As for what he can see, if he wanted

he could describe a field of white, perhaps
a field of white flowers, of snow, of sand
with no tracks or interruptions, nothing to show
usage or the casual depredations of man.

SPIDER WEB

There are stories that unwind themselves as simply
as a ball of string. A man is on a plane between
New York and Denver. He sees his life
as moving along a straight line. Today here,
tomorrow there. The destination is not so
important as the progression itself. During lunch
he talks to the woman seated beside him.
She is from Baltimore, perhaps twenty years older.
It turns out she has had two children killed
by drunk drivers, two incidents fifteen
years apart. At first I wanted to die every day,
she says, now I only want to die now and then.
Again and again, she tries to make her life
move forward in a straight line but it keeps
curving back to those two deaths, curves back
like a fishhook stuck through her gut. I guess
I'm lucky, she says, I have other children left.
The man and woman discuss books, horses; they
talk about different cities; but each conversation
keeps returning to the fact of those deaths,
as if each conversation were a fall from a roof
and those two deaths were the ground itself—
a son and daughter, one five, one fourteen.
The plane lands, they separate. The man goes off
to his various meetings, but for several days
whenever he's at dinner or sitting around
in the evening, he says to whomever he is with,
You know, I met the saddest woman on the plane.
But he can't get it right, can't decide whether
she is sad or brave or what, can't describe
how the woman herself fought to keep the subject
straight, keep it from bending back to the fact
of the dead children, and then how she would
collapse and weep, then curse herself and
go at it again. After a week or so, the man

completes his work and returns home. Once more
he gathers up the threads of his life.
It's spring. The man works in his garden,
repairs all that is broken around his house.
He thinks of how a spider makes its web;
how the web is torn by people with brooms,
insects, rapacious birds; how the spider
rebuilds and rebuilds, until the wind
takes the web and breaks it and flicks it
into heaven's blue and innocent immensity.

FUNERAL

When her coffin had been carried from the room,
the house remained exactly as she had arranged it—
her thoughts present in the position of each chair,
in the snapshots of the dead upon the mantel;
and by the kitchen door a smudge where her hand
had often rested. Her grandson, by himself
in the house, drags a chair over to that spot,
climbs up and just touches his tongue to the mark,
and in its salt and faint taste of cinnamon
a hundred bright occasions return to him.
With his eyes shut and his tongue pressed to the wood,
he can feel the house unfurl its wings, rise up
and glide over the fields of wheat and small farms
like a horned owl from the branch of a dead tree.
His heart quickens with excitement. No telling
where he is going, and will she be waiting?

LOUD MUSIC

My stepdaughter and I circle round and round.
You see, I like the music loud, the speakers
throbbing, jam-packing the room with sound whether
Bach or rock and roll, the volume cranked up so
each bass note is like a hand smacking the gut.
But my stepdaughter disagrees. She is four
and likes the music decorous, pitched below
her own voice—that tenuous projection of self.
With music blasting, she feels she disappears,
is lost within the blare, which in fact I like.
But at four what she wants is self-location
and uses her voice as a porpoise uses
its sonar: to find herself in all this space.
If she had a sort of box with a peephole
and looked inside, what she'd like to see would be
herself standing there in her red pants, jacket,
yellow plastic lunch box: a proper subject
for serious study. But me, if I raised
the same box to my eye, I would wish to find
the ocean on one of those days when wind
and thick cloud make the water gray and restless
as if some huge creature brooded underneath,
a rocky coast with a road along the shore
where someone like me was walking and has gone.
Loud music does this, it wipes out the ego,
leaving turbulent water and winding road,
a landscape stripped of people and language—
how clear the air becomes, how sharp the colors.

FACES

My daughter baby Clio lies on her back
on the sheepskin rug, jerking her arms and feet
like a turtle stuck upside down in the dirt
struggling to get up. But here there is no threat,
I tell myself. The room is benign and I
act for the best. She is just contentedly
wriggling. It is nothing like a turtle flipped
over while two or three crows sidle closer,
eager to pluck her soft parts. The room is safe
and I direct my life to keep it like that.
How much is this a fiction I believe in?
We are forced to live in a place without walls
and I build her shelter with bits of paper.
The ever attentive beaks surround us. These
birds are her future—face of a teacher, face
of a thief, one with the face of her father.

PARACHUTES

He'd not known he loved her so he let her go.
You know those movies where a bunch of soldiers
jump out the back of a plane? That's how she looked,
falling away through scattered clouds, a dark speck
getting smaller, then nothing. He turned aside.
He felt a squeezing, a pain in his chest, but
he told himself it was nothing. He made up
another life, had some good times, bad times.
Always there was this squeezing but he felt sure
it meant nothing. He built himself a new house,
family; he tried to make his way in the world
as one makes little figurines out of clay,
clay women and children, clay automobiles,
a clay dog to fetch his paper, clay slippers.
Move, he said to the figurines, jump through hoops.
He kept remembering how she'd disappeared
like someone tumbling from the back of a plane.
You know the movie—it's Germany and wartime.
The parachutes drifting down like milkweed seeds
in the rising sun—that's what she looked like,
falling through cloud, a dark speck getting smaller.
Wasn't this the old trouble with adult life,
wasn't there always damage and destruction—
like looking at a wartime landscape, the wrecked
villages, plundered fields, the roads shot to hell?
Sometimes it felt reversed and he was down there
with his little clay life watching the figurines
get blasted to bits. The planes would disappear,
distant specks of silver. He'd see the wreckage,
dead animals, busted machines. This is my life,
he would think, this is what I've made for myself.
Although the sun was rising, the clock had stopped,
the season stopped. The day wasn't beginning,
it had ended. In the sky, there was nothing,

no parachutes or planes, not even birds, just
a vacancy; that's what the pain was, the squeezing,
this absence like the sky itself inside him.

MARSYAS, MIDAS, AND THE BARBER

The duel between Marsyas and Apollo was one of those
historical things—flute versus strings, peasants
versus roving noblemen. Marsyas had found the pipes
near a stream and since they almost seemed to play
themselves he gave himself up to the pleasure. Then,
when he saw he had talent, he thought, Why not
be tops? He was a domesticated satyr with ambitions,
a little fellow who wanted to be a big fellow,
whose one admirer in high places was King Midas,
who liked his low jokes and easy way with women.
Nobody had looked at him until he found the flute;
he was too fat, too lazy. Even with the flute they only
paid attention when he played, so he played all the time,
until Apollo appeared and said, You must think you're
pretty hot. Even then Marsyas couldn't stay shut up,
mostly because the peasants kept bobbing their heads,
begging him to show this big fellow just what a hot
ticket he really was, and even Midas nodded
encouragingly and backed the local boy over the star.
But it should be said that the contest that followed
had nothing to do with music. It was all about
brain power, and there Apollo beat him flat. Whatever
made Marsyas think he could sing and play the pipes
at the same time? Could he sing with his nose, blow
with his ears? And so he lost both the contest
and his skin, which Apollo ripped from his body
like a sock from a foot. Then it was Midas's turn
to bear the brunt of divine attention with the god
standing above him asking unpleasant questions.
Did Midas really think Marsyas the better musician?
Shuffling his feet, scratching his chin, Midas
had never been known for the wisdom of his decisions—
just look at his trouble with food turning to gold.
But, yes, despite threats and dire consequences
he would stand up for Marsyas; the flute had defeated

the lyre. But Apollo had no use for Midas's loyalty
and so the mortal's insolence was ironically punished.
You think you've got good ears, buster? Try hearing
with these. How dreadful to find his once normal ears
had been turned into a pair of floppy ones covered
with silky brown fur. Tugging at one as it dangled
near the level of his chin, Midas probably caught
a glimpse of his future—bleak for himself, funny
for everyone else. Was it worth it? Did he recant?
If given a second chance, would he shout, Marsyas,
what a bum, no tact, no talent, and no technique!
But lucky for us history gives no second chances
or consider the bravery that might go unrepeated—
Horatio dodging the bridge, Crockett missing the Alamo.
The necessity is to act from your essential nature,
and Midas, though foolish, was loyal. Even Marsyas,
a near nobody, was fated to be true to his instrument.
And Midas's barber—you see how these stories descend
to their lowest denominators—even the barber,
who had been warned to keep his mouth shut or else,
was at a loss to obey, being naturally talkative.
How could he be expected to keep such a secret?
So he spoke it to a hole in the ground and soon
all the grass was saying, King Midas has ass's ears.
At the very moment of his execution, did the barber
still think he'd ever had the ability to keep silent?
And Midas, now that the entire country knew about
his unfortunate deformity, could he stand up
and tell the world that Marsyas was a no-talent bum?
And Marsyas, as he wandered through the woods
wondering why he had so few friends, when he saw
the flute and picked it up, if somebody smart
had rushed up to tell him the nature of his future,
would he have dropped the flute and turned aside?

He was a little artist who wanted to be a big artist.
Had he been able to see his skin nailed to the tree
would he have denied the dancers, the cheering crowds,
in favor of a long life and anonymity forever?

PONY EXPRESS

For Mary Karr

Some would have you think the Pony Express
is dead. Don't believe it. They're only waiting.
You know the letter you thought of writing
to that woman you once loved, the one describing
how you remembered her hair or hands or
the curve of her chin? That's the sort of letter
they now deal in, and if you wrote it,
they would show up to take it. These days
the riders like apologies, regrets, the letters
that begin: If only I had known then
what I know now—these aged men with their
aged ponies, playing cards and polishing
their saddles in the city's only livery stable,
waiting for someone's change of heart.
Take the example of the old clerk who lives
by himself in a cheap room. Forty years ago
he loved a woman and now he dreams of her face.
If only he wrote, Sometimes, I think of you;
sometimes, I still desire you; sometimes,
I wish I could hear you laugh once again.
Then suddenly there would appear at the door
a frail old man in a cowboy hat and gunfighter
mustache. He'd take that letter and, oh,
he would ride. He'd gallop his pony across
highways, expressways, railways, even
airport runways until at last he reached
the cottage of a bright-cheeked old woman
who would read the letter with one hand pressed
to her heart as the sunset twinkled and
from somewhere came the twittering of violins.
But of course the old clerk won't write the letter,
and as the world gets colder, he gets smaller;
and as the world gets harder, he gets meaner.
At night he perches over his hot plate
watching the sun collapse behind the high rises,

while across the city a last Pony Express rider
sticks his head from the stable door to see what
final shenanigans the setting sun is up to.
Why is it, they both think, that some days the sun
just seems to flash out as if someone had snatched
up its last light and smashed it to the ground?

CHARITY

What is charity but doing something
you don't have to do, not for yourself,
not for anybody; or maybe you do it
just for the taste of meanness in it?
Bored and restless, five whores lean back
on a long red couch. Four wear flouncy
blue blouses; the one in the middle
wears a black dress open to the waist.
Behind them, the red paisley wallpaper
looks like amoebas mating, a warning
of how to get the clap. A man enters.
He's short and dressed in a suit. Perhaps
he's fifty. They guess he's a clerk.
He's tired of hearing his wife snore,
tired of women who don't look back.
He picks the woman in black and she
takes him to her room. On the table
as a joke she keeps a small guillotine
just big enough for a finger. No one
ever looks. She strokes him, touches him
with her mouth. Nothing will make him hard.
The man feels terrible. Never mind,
says the whore, I'll read you a story
instead. She makes him sit on the bed
and reads him a story about a dog
that jumps into a river to save two
small boys. It's winter. There's a waterfall.
The dog gets them both. As the whore reads,
her breasts sway lazily above the clerk.
Isn't that amazing? she says at last.
When the clerk leaves, she charges him double.
I don't do that for everyone, she tells him.
The whore makes a lot of noise washing herself,
then walks back to the couch. Sometimes it's
the little guys who have the biggest pricks,
she tells the others, don't I feel stuffed.

THE GENERAL
AND THE TANGO SINGER

Some people put their trust in art, others
believe in murder. Each can be in error.
Take the example of the general and the tango
singer who go to a restaurant for dinner.
They are both big men and they are starving,
so they order a five-course meal beginning
with clams casino. Then they settle down to discuss
the nature of beauty. For the tango singer,
beauty means submission to the rule of objects.
For the general, it means force—the beauty
of a mailed fist. Suddenly the owner
bursts through the door shouting, Fire, Fire.
The stockroom is in flames. He must get help.
Look no farther, says the general, I can put
the fire out. And if he can't, says the tango
singer, then I can—bring us the turtle soup.
The two friends eat the soup and talk about truth.
For the general, truth is the ability
to whip your ideas forward to victory.
For the singer, it means knowing when to give in.
The owner appears again; the whole back
of the restaurant is burning. Forget it,
says the tango singer, we'll fix it in a minute—
bring us the salmon soufflé. And more wine,
says the general, we need more wine. They eat
and drink and talk about art. For the singer,
art consists of synthesis and compromise.
For the general, it's a total assault
on the senses—something like a punch in the nose.
The owner again comes running. He is crying.
The fire has reached the kitchen. There'll be
no more food tonight. With the air of men
for whom duty is a harsh mistress, the general
and tango singer prepare to put out the blaze.
Such a nuisance, says the general. Such a bore,

says the singer. The fire appears at the door.
Talk about starving, roars the fire, I am really
ravenous. The general tells everyone
to stand back. Then he takes out his pistol
and shoots six bullets into the flames.
Yum, yum, says the fire, I adore hot lead.
Now it is my turn, says the tango singer.
He begins to sing one of his very own songs—
When my baby ran off with Big Leo,
I cut off her feet and threw them in the trash.
The music splashes over the fire, which
gobbles up each note before sweeping forward
through the restaurant, devouring tables,
chairs, the white tablecloths, devouring
even the plates. Everyone rushes out
to the street. The restaurant is destroyed.
You said you could save it, cries the owner.
The general and tango singer shrug their shoulders.
That was not a real fire, they say, a real
fire would have begged for mercy. We cannot
be held responsible for frauds. The general
and the tango singer stroll off down the street.
Did you see how it hesitated when I shot it?
Did you see how it paused when I sang?
Both are very pleased. They talk about the confused
state of the world. When will it ever get better?
These problems won't be solved in our lifetime,
says the general, yet how fortunate for those future
generations to have their road made clear. Yes,
says the tango singer, that lucky time will come
like a gentle caress. I beg to differ, says
the general, it will come like a bust in the jaw.
Behind them the fire listens to their talk
as it picks over the restaurant as if over
a plate of bones. It knows how the future will come,

no one knows better. And if its mouth were not
too full to speak, it would gladly tell. How sweet
will be that future time when night will burn
as bright as day, when each cold corner receives
the precious gift of warmth and even the smallest
fire toddles off to dreamland on a full stomach.

CEMETERY NIGHTS II

Because the moon burns a bright orange,
because their memories beat them like flails,
because even in death it is possible
to take only so much, because the night
watchman has slipped out for a drink,
the dead decide to have a party. Helter-skelter,
they hurry to the center of the graveyard,
clasp hands and attack the possibility
of pleasure. How brave to play the clarinet
when your fingers fall off. How persevering to dance
when your feet keep fleeing into the tall grass.
How courageous to sing when your tongue flops down
on the stage and you must stop to stick it back.
And what does she sing, this chanteuse of the night,
Melancholy Baby? I Got Plenty of Nothing?

Where we have come from we'll soon forget.
Where we are going is the dust at our feet.
Where we are now is the best we can expect.

Slim pickings, says a crow to his buddy.
Just wait 'til the world flips over, says the other,
then we'll eat until our stomachs burst.
In a nearby bar the night watchman says, They can't
keep me down, I'm going places, I got plans.
The bartender yawns and glances from the window.
Some great bird is flapping across the face of the moon.
He thinks, Whatever happened to Jenny Whatshername?
Car crash, cancer, killer in the night? He remembers
once watching her pee in the woods, how she just
squatted down and pulled up her pink dress.
For fifteen cents she let him see her crack.
So white it looked, the wound that would never heal;
then how pink when she had delicately

spread it apart with two fingers. Excitedly,
he had galloped through the woods waving a stick,
hitting trees, clumps of earth; seeking marauders,
Indians, pirates to kill just to protect her.

MERMAID

When are we satisfied or get what we want,
when do we speak the truth of our feelings?
A man has been rude to the rich and powerful.
Magicians are called in. After much talk,
they decide to put him inside a tree. The man
wakes up. It's dark. He discovers he's trapped
inside a black walnut but it takes many years
to understand this. He becomes accustomed
to the touch of birds' feet, the touch of wind
and change of seasons, but to his suffering
and sense of loss he becomes accustomed
never. Oh, how he misses his loved ones.
Then, by good fortune, a local sculptor cuts
down the black walnut to make a figurehead
for a nearby tavern. The man trapped inside
believes that in this new shape he might
at last be able to express his pain and
frustrated longing. Stoically, he endures
the tap of the hammer, bite of the chisel.
Although the sculptor is one of the world's
ten million bad artists, he successfully
turns the tree into a mermaid with golden
hair, pendulous breasts, and scarlet nipples.
The man inside looks out through the mermaid's
bright blue eyes and in a mirror he sees how
his suffering has been transformed into
the alluring invitation of the mermaid's curves.
The sculptor has taken the man's desire
for his wife and changed it into a twinkle
in the mermaid's eye. He has taken the man's
pride and turned it into the mermaid's grin.
He has taken his rebellion and reshaped it
into the upward thrust of the mermaid's breasts.
How easily does artifice transform true feeling.
Yet how strongly does feeling continue to struggle.

Months pass, years go by. On windy nights,
the mermaid swings from her double chain
so the links chafe and rub, making a sound
like a creaking door, and in that noise the man
trapped in the wood puts all his unhappiness.
What a gloomy sound, say the men returning from work,
mechanics and carpenters, the men from the mines,
and they hurry into the tavern and order their beer,
and there among the smoke and laughter, one lifts
his glass and drinks to the future. But as he speaks
the word, he hears the creaking of the chain
and briefly he sees himself feeling his way
down a tunnel deep in the mountain, lost with
no light and no friends and no sense of an end
to his own unique but not uncommon story.

MY TOWN

This happens occasionally in my town. Maybe
it's a sort of nervousness or hysteria, even
displaced fervor, as if fervor were a kind
of cloud or the fog that rolls in to envelop
the coast, that warm August fog, really more
of a bandage than a fog. You see how I stumble.

It begins with a man running onto his neighbor's
front porch. Come on, he shouts, let's go!
His neighbor hurries out and the two of them
run down the street shouting, It's coming!
Then another man joins them, maybe a woman,
and from other houses come more men and women,
some pulling on coats or sweaters. It's coming!
they shout, and their voices seem eager.
Soon there are maybe twenty people; a man
is buckling his belt, one woman as she runs
is taking the yellow curlers from her hair.
They run onto porches, hammer on doors. Now
the street is getting full. It's like a river,
little streams emerging from separate houses.
There's the guy who cuts my hair, the checkout
girl from Jack's Quik Shop. Let's go! they shout,
and their faces shine as if just washed, as if their
eagerness had erased all other concerns—the baker
who went bankrupt, the wife of the town drunk—
their faces empty of all but anticipation, like
blank paper waiting to be used, or new clothing,
anything ready to be taken up for the first time.
Past the high school and park, brushing the swings
that flop back and forth on their chains. It's
coming, they shout—a huge crowd and all on foot.

It's the oldsters who stop first, halting
to catch their breath; then the kids for whom

it's half a joke; then others. In twos and threes,
they come to a stop, sometimes far in the country
as dogs run barking along the side of the road.
Those in good shape can keep it up for miles but
then they too are forced to halt until there's
just one, the town cop or high school track star,
sprinting ahead with arms outstretched. It's coming,
he shouts. But soon he also stops, and almost
with embarrassment he begins to make his way back.
They all come back, not looking at each other
or talking. By now it's getting late. Going
into their houses, they pull down their shades,
turn out the lights so you would think there was
no one at home, although you know they are still
hopeful and stand listening in darkened rooms,
waiting for the next time when someone bursts
from his house shouting, Let's go! Which makes me
curious about other places, other lives. We must
get to the bottom of these mysteries, discover
what people require to be happy. Otherwise
we proceed in chaos and confusion, like someone
throwing a bunch of confetti into the air: some
blows north, some south, and some we never know.

THE INVITATION

There are lives in which nothing goes right.
The would-be suicide takes a bottle of pills
and immediately throws up. He tries
to hang himself but gets his arm caught
in the noose. He tries to throw himself
under a subway but misses the last train.
He walks home. It is raining. He catches a cold
and dies. Once in heaven it is no better.
He mops the marble staircase and accidentally
jams his foot in the pail. All his harp strings
break. His halo slips down over his neck
and nearly chokes him. Why is he here?
demands one of the noble dead, an archbishop
or general, a leader of men: If a loser
like that can enter heaven, then how is it
an honor for us to be here as well—
those of us who are totally deserving?
But the would-be suicide knows none of this.
In the evening, he returns to his little cloud house
and watches the sun set over the planet Earth.
He stares down at the cities filled with people
and thinks how sad it is that they should
rush backwards and forwards as if they had
some great destination when their only
destination is death itself—a place
to be reached by sitting as well as running.
He thinks about his own life with its
betrayals and disappointments. Regret, regret—
how he never made a softball team, how his
favorite shirts always shrank in the wash.
His eyes moisten and he sheds a few tears, but
secretly, because in heaven crying is forbidden.
Still, the tears tumble down through all those layers
of blue sky and strike a salesman rushing
between Point A and Point B. The salesman slips,

staggers, and stops as if slapped in the face.
People on the street think he's crazy or drunk.
Why am I selling ten thousand ballpoint pens?
he asks himself. Suddenly his only wish is to
dance the tango. He sees how the setting sun
caresses the cold faces of the buildings.
He sees a beautiful woman and desperately wants
to ask her to stroll in the park. Maybe he will
kiss her cheek; maybe she will love him back.
You maniac, she tells him, didn't you know
I was only waiting for you to ask me?

STREET CORNER ROMANCE

For Karin Ash

There is nothing, no snippet of flesh, no dead chunk
of refuse that can't be saved and made of use.
So at the hospital they've collected all the cut off
parts and have fashioned themselves a little man—
stomach of a diplomat, feet of a pimp, eyes
of an equestrienne. What a joke for the interns,
terror for the nurses—shoulders of a ditch digger,
heart of a piano player, while for his soul they've got
a twelve-volt battery. They name him Jack and one night
Jack is sent out to buy beer—kidneys of a banker,
ears of a buffoon. He toddles toward the corner bar
with a handful of change, dressed in a green scrub
suit and pulling a wagon with his twelve-volt soul.
Halfway down the block he stops at a parking meter.
I'm Jack, says the little man and waits for an answer—
liver of a teacher, tongue of a railway conductor.
I'm Jack, says the little man to the parking meter.
He's not more than five feet tall and one leg
is a foot shorter than the other. He reaches out
and strokes the parking meter's smooth metal head.
What's your name? says the little man. His twelve-volt
soul is humming—toes of a dancer, knees of a killer.
How can I make you happy? asks the little man and puts
a quarter in the slot. Softly, the parking meter
begins to tick. I love you, says the little man,
as steam escapes from his discount battery.
You are all I have ever wanted—pancreas
of a dentist, bladder of a house painter. He puts
his hand behind the meter's head and gently tugs.
The meter appears to resist. Come link your hopes
to mine—testicles of a piccolo player, rib cage
of a thief. My life is nothing without you.
The parking meter remains rooted to the spot,
passively gulping down quarters while
traffic whirls by and people walk their dogs.

When the little man returns to the hospital,
it's on a stretcher. He's spent all his money
and there are tire tracks across his middle. Sure,
he threw himself under a bus. What did they
expect, sending a newborn into the night despite
the age and wisdom of his various parts? They're
just lucky he didn't go crazy for a Mack truck.
Then what a dance he would have led the doctors
as he and his beloved consummated their marriage
on the city streets—tearing up the asphalt,
knocking down the cops. You see, we are no good
in emotional isolation. Even a tire iron yearns
for a steely mate, and love, what is love but
that dark reflecting lake that any creature
may have the good or ill-fortune to glance into.

SPIRITUAL CHICKENS

A man eats a chicken every day for lunch,
and each day the ghost of another chicken
joins the crowd in the dining room. If he could
only see them! Hundreds and hundreds of spiritual
chickens, sitting on chairs, tables, covering
the floor, jammed shoulder to shoulder. At last
there is no more space and one of the chickens
is popped back across the spiritual plain to the earthly.
The man is in the process of picking his teeth.
Suddenly there's a chicken at the end of the table,
strutting back and forth, not looking at the man
but knowing he is there, as is the way with chickens.
The man makes a grab for the chicken but his hand
passes right through her. He tries to hit the chicken
with a chair and the chair passes through her.
He calls in his wife but she can see nothing.
This is his own private chicken, even if he
fails to recognize her. How is he to know
this is a chicken he ate seven years ago
on a hot and steamy Wednesday in July,
with a little tarragon, a little sour cream?
The man grows afraid. He runs out of his house
flapping his arms and making peculiar hops
until the authorities take him away for a cure.
Faced with the choice between something odd
in the world or something broken in his head,
he opts for the broken head. Certainly,
this is safer than putting his opinions
in jeopardy. Much better to think he had
imagined it, that he had made it happen.
Meanwhile, the chicken struts back and forth
at the end of the table. Here she was, jammed in
with the ghosts of six thousand dead hens, when
suddenly she has the whole place to herself.
Even the nervous man has disappeared. If she

had a brain, she would think she had caused it.
She would grow vain, egotistical, she would
look for someone to fight, but being a chicken
she can just enjoy it and make little squawks,
silent to all except the man who ate her,
who is far off banging his head against a wall
like someone trying to repair a leaky vessel,
making certain that nothing unpleasant gets in
or nothing of value falls out. How happy
he would have been to be born a chicken,
to be of good use to his fellow creatures
and rich in companionship after death.
As it is he is constantly being squeezed
between the world and his idea of the world.
Better to have a broken head—why surrender
his corner on truth?—better just to go crazy.

WOLVES IN THE STREET

Tonight the world wishes to intrude itself
between our nakedness and one desire.
I climb from bed, walk to the window. Wolves prowl
back and forth between the houses and parked cars.
In their jaws they carry pieces of what they
have captured, sometimes a hand, sometimes a foot.
You lie uncovered on white sheets. I study
your breasts, your thin waist. I try to tell myself
your body is all I have ever wanted.
How long before the world overwhelms us?
You turn toward me, your lips move, wanting to speak.
In the ornate mirror above the bureau,
I see my teeth and snout, my small yellow eyes.
I cannot hear your words for all the barking.

LEARNING TO THINK

My stepdaughter tells of voices in her head,
ones that say Yes and No and tell her stories.
Soon I realize she has begun to think
and I remember when the talking started
in my own head. It was a summer morning.
I was four and in bed at my grandparents'.
Suddenly I was aware of these voices
inside me, inside my own body, voices
calmly detailing my plans for the day
where earlier there had been only silence.
In that moment the world felt so different
that I jumped from bed and ran to the mirror
to see if my face too had changed, was older,
wiser, more controlled. But no, it was my face
I found waiting there, the same as yesterday,
same as tomorrow, and although disappointed,
the world was still fresh, that time when its wonders
outweighed its shortcomings; and propelled forward
by this new mystery, I hurried downstairs.
What did I think to find there? An adult world
eager to share in my discoveries, what else
was possible in that happy place before
the arrival of cynicism and doubt,
those further steps on the way to adulthood.

THE WORDS WE HAVE SPOKEN

At first they look like rocks or pieces of glass,
anything that's been sharpened or has a point—
shards of pottery, broken sticks. But really
they are teeth stretching from one side of the valley
to the other. Where did they come from? we wonder.
They are ours. These are the words we have spoken
in anger, thrown at each other in attack
or defense, and now they form a barrier.
Can we get around them? I don't know the way.
I think of you on the other side, lonely
and as unhappy as I am; but possibly
you are content in a room with white walls,
flowering plants, a room where I might even
be welcome could I discover the right roads.
From my side of the valley, I see darkness
climbing the distant hills. It is getting late.
We have to learn to save ourselves, change ourselves,
or else we'll come to a time when love won't help—
night of no welcome, night of the long indifference.

EBB TIDE

In early morning there were gulls that arrived
to make their cries repeatedly above his house.
He thought of the people who'd died in the night,
their final moments, the panic and fumbling
for a switch, the slipping away. At this hour
even the highway is silent, the one noise
being a neighbor trying to start his car,
the grinding and grinding of the motor. This
is when his life feels most fragile, when each part
of the world he believed important trembles
like a shadow puppet on a wall—a bird
or dog to coax a child to sleep. No sleep now,
or at least until he reenters the lie
of his life. He thinks of his children asleep
in their beds. He reaches out but does not touch
the long curve of his wife's back. He sees himself
above his body, staring down at the sprawl
that he and his woman make. Given the world
and its accidents, what brought them together?
They resemble two boats, two trawlers lying
hull to hull, waiting out the ebb in green light.
From inside he hears the murmur of voices,
quiet laughter. The sun heats the rusted metal.
Then comes the abrupt cry of gulls to wake him.
Which is the dream and which the journey? He needs
to free himself from the net of confusion
that binds him. Light breaks over the window sill.
It's summer. It's time to regather his life.
He swings his feet, sets them firmly on the floor.
The day, he thinks, will be another hot one.

ORPHEUS

Immediately on emerging from the dark tunnel
to hell, Orpheus began to kick at the earth
and curse Eurydice for her betrayal. She knew
he was weak. She knew he could refuse her nothing.
Why had she begged to see his face? Squatting down,
he pressed his mouth to the mouth of the hole.
Why have I let you break my heart? he shouted.
He thought of her smug, self-satisfied smile
when he had turned and taken his last look at her,
knowing they were lost, that their story was over.
Still, for weeks he lingered around that hole
in the earth with its smell of decay and the vast
murmur of the dead like the murmur of the sea,
unable to eat, unable to play the lyre.
Other women came, but he ignored them.
They offered themselves, but he refused them.
See us as Eurydice, they asked. Impossible,
he said, you are too different. Show us, they said.
He described how her hair fell over one shoulder.
Like that, he said, but yours is the wrong color.
Show us, they answered. So they changed the color
of their hair. Then he taught them how to dress,
how to walk, how to make up their faces until
once more she stood before him and his grief
overswept his heart. Come with us, they said.
But Orpheus still wasn't ready. Walk after me,
he told them, beg me to look at your faces.
So they began their journey across the country—
Orpheus first, then the dozen Thracian women.
Orpheus, they cried, look at us, look at our faces.
But Orpheus felt no temptation to turn.
He raised his lyre and began to play.
He strode along and the women hurried to catch up,
stumbling and hurting themselves on the stones.
Orpheus, they cried, turn and look at us.

We are Eurydice. Louder, he said, cry louder.
The women raised their voices and he pretended
not to hear them. He was filled with confidence.
I'll go back, he thought, I'll return to hell.

What else could the women do but destroy him?
They were sick to death of his endless strumming.
They grew berserk and before he could say Stop
or There has been a mistake, they tore him apart
and threw the pieces into the River Hebrus. How
soothing the silence felt. How wonderful to view
the horizon without the insult of his indifferent back.
They returned to their lives, got married, grew fat.
They forgot about Orpheus and the indiscretions
of their youth, or perhaps they remembered a time
when there had been a light or maybe a noise
and it had grown too loud or maybe too bright.
Whatever the case, they had brushed it aside.
Orpheus's lyre washed up on the shores of Lesbos,
where it was put in a temple for safekeeping.
One night, years later, a wealthy young man
crept into the temple meaning to play a few songs.
He had a girlfriend he wanted to impress.
He had no sense of the danger, no sense
of the power of the instrument. He touched
the strings. Eurydice, they cried, Eurydice.
The sound was like a wind that flattens wheat.
It swept through the city, driving animals crazy.
From every street, dogs raced toward the temple,
snarling and biting at themselves in frenzy,
scrambling over each other's backs through the doorway.
As the Thracian women had killed Orpheus,
so the dogs devoured the foolish young man.
What else could they have done, being earthborn,
but slaughter what had pricked their creature hearts?

MISSED CHANCES

In the city of missed chances, the streetlights
always flicker, the second hand clothing shops
stay open all night and used furniture stores
employ famous greeters. This is where you
are sent after that moment of hesitation.
You were too slow to act, too afraid to jump,
too shy or uncertain to speak up. Do you recall
the moment? Your finger was raised, your mouth
open, and then, strangely, silence. Now you walk
past men and women wrapped in the memory
of the speeches they should have uttered—
Over my dead body. Sure, I'd be happy with
ten thousand. If you walk out, don't come back—
past dogs practicing faster bites, cowboys
with faster draws, where even the cockroach
knows that next time he'll jump to the left.
You were simply going to say, Don't go, or words
to that effect—Don't go, don't leave, don't walk
out of my life. Nothing fancy, nothing to stutter
about. Now you're shouting it every ten seconds.

In the city of missed chances, it is always just past
sunset and the freeways are jammed with people
driving to homes they regret ever choosing,
where wives or helpmates have burned the dinner,
where the TV's blown a fuse and even the dog,
tied to a post in the backyard, feels confused,
uncertain, and makes tentative barks at the moon.
How easy to say it—Don't go, don't leave, don't
disappear. Now you've said it a million times.
You even stroll over to the Never-Too-Late
Tattoo Parlor and have it burned into the back
of your hand, right after the guy who had
Don't shoot, Madge, printed big on his forehead.
Then you go down to the park, where you discover

a crowd of losers, your partners in hesitation,
standing nose to nose with the bronze statues
repeating the phrases engraved on their hearts—
Let me kiss you. Don't hit me. I love you—
while the moon pretends to take it all in.
Let's get this straight once and for all:
is that a face up there or is it a rabbit, and if
it's a face, then why does it hold itself back,
why doesn't it take control and say, Who made
this mess, who's responsible? But this is no time
for rebellion, you must line up with the others,
then really start to holler, Don't go, don't go—
like a hammer sinking chains into concrete,
like doors slamming and locking one after another,
like a heart beats when it's scared half to death.

WHITE THIGHS

White thighs like slices of white cake—
three pre-teenage girls on a subway
talking excitedly about what they will
see and do and buy downtown, while near them
a man stares, then pulls back to look
at the slash and jab of the graffiti.
He sees himself as trying to balance
on the peak of a steep metal roof
but once again he turns to watch
the girls in their grown-up dresses,
their eye shadow and painted mouths. How
white the skin must be on the insides
of their thighs. He can almost taste
their heat and he imagines his teeth
pressed to the humid flesh until once more
he jerks back his head like yanking
a dog on a leash, until he sees his face
in the glass, gray and middle-aged. The night,
he thinks, the night—meaning not simply
night-time but those hours before dawn
when he feels his hunger as if it were
a great hulking creature in the hallway
outside his door, some beast of darkness.
And again he feels his head beginning
to twist on its hateful stalk. White thighs—
to trip or slip on that steep metal roof:
his final capitulation to the dark.

THE FACE IN THE CEILING

A man comes home to find his wife in bed
with the milkman. They're really going at it.
The man yanks the milkman off by his heels
so his chin hits the floor. Then he gets his gun.
It looks like trouble for all concerned.
Why is modern life so complicated?
The wife and milkman scramble into their clothes.
The man makes them sit at the kitchen table,
takes all but one bullet out of the gun,
then spins the cylinder. We'll let fate decide,
he says. For the sake of symmetry, he gets their
mongrel dog and makes him sit at the table as well.
The dog is glad to oblige but fears the worst.
North, south, east, west, says the man, who's the one
that God likes best? He puts the gun to his head
and pulls the trigger. Click. Whew, what a relief.
Spinning the cylinder, he aims the gun at his wife.
North, south, east, west, he says and again pulls
the trigger. Another click. He spins the cylinder
and aims at the milkman. North, south, east, west.
A third click. He points the gun at the dog, who is
scratching fitfully at his collar. North, south,
east, west, who do you think God likes best?
The man pulls the trigger. Bang! He's killed the dog.
Good grief, says the wife, he was just a pup.
They look down at the sprawled body of the dog
and are so struck by the mean-spiritedness
of the world's tricks that they can do nothing
but go out for a pizza and something to drink.
When they have finished eating, the man says,
You take my wife home, I'm sorry I was selfish.
And the milkman says, No, you take her home,
I'm sorry I was greedy. And the wife says,
Let's all go home together. A little later
they are lying side by side on the double bed

completely dressed and shyly holding hands.
They stare up at the ceiling, where they think
they see God's face in the ridges of shadow,
the swirls of plaster and paint. It looks like
the kid who first punched me in the nose,
says the husband. It looks like the fellow
who fired me from my first job, says the milkman.
And the wife remembers once as a child
a man who called her over to his car,
and opening the door she saw he was naked
from his waist down to his red sneakers.
What makes you think that God likes anyone?
asks the wife. Wide awake, the three of them
stare at the ceiling trying to define the kind
of face they find there until the sun comes up
and pushes away the shadow, and then it no longer
matters whether the face is good or evil, generous
or small-minded. So they get up, feeling sheepish,
and don't look at each other as they wash and
brush their teeth and drink a cup of coffee,
then go out and make their way in the world,
neither too badly nor too well as is the case
with compromises, sneaking along walls, dashing
across streets. You think it is nothing to risk
your life every day of the great struggle until
what you hold most precious is torn from you?
How loudly the traffic roars, how ferociously
the great machines bear down upon them
and how courageous it is for them to be there.

CEMETERY NIGHTS III

There had been complaints, dissatisfactions,
even harsh words. An angel was dispatched.
He was a mere functionary, the wrong
person in the wrong place at the wrong time.
He knew he had no chance of success and
dawdled along the way. Once in the cemetery
he stood perfectly still on a small pillar.
He hoped the dead would think him a statue,
a symbol of their faith in a better future.
Maybe he moved or cleared his throat.
In any case, the dead soon gathered round—
dead bus drivers, dead schoolteachers, dead doctors.
Why should they throw only rocks? They threw
chunks of their own flesh. They threw hands.
They threw armbones, legbones. They bounced
their skulls off the head of the unhappy angel.
For the maggots it was a real treat, flying
through the air like that, an airborne picnic.

At last the angel felt he had helped them enough
and he returned with his failure to heaven.
In a park, a boy and girl lay naked in the grass.
They saw the angel limping home through the sky—
a bright spark against the pallor of the moon—
and guessed it was a piece of space-age technology.
Even as people sleep, said the boy, scientists
are working to make the world a better place.
If I'm pregnant, said the girl, I'll name the baby
Flash, if it's male; Star, if it's female.
She imagined her baby addressing the United Nations,
just like Jesus before the teachers in the temple.
With renewed hope the delegates run out to the street.
The sun would be bright purple, something weird.
Right away, the blind stop banging into lampposts,
cripples would dance the snake dance like crazy.

THE APPRENTICE

If man has a soul and that soul has value
then it stands to reason that some creature
would want more than one, which was just
the case of the inadequate angel promoted
to apprentice devil who hurried to earth
to find someone to tempt. What could he offer?
That your toast would land jelly-side-up;
that your keys would be in whatever pocket
you reached for; that you would never again
be stopped by a red light. Landing in New York,
he was at once so successful that by the end
of a week he had packed off to hell two
taxi drivers and a cripple, but then
he raised his sights to the owner of a Greek
restaurant on the Upper West Side and everything
ground to a halt. His soul seemed so sweet.
I listen to string quartets, the owner said.
I give bums free slices of spinach quiche.
And the devil imagined a soul made entirely
of pink nougat and twice the size of a brick.
The only trouble was the owner worked sixteen
hours a day and had no time to hear any offers.
The devil would sip mint tea as the owner
polished the silver. You know, said the owner,
I often help old ladies across the street,
I even march in anti-vivisectionist parades.
It was then the devil heard himself saying,
Let me help you with these dishes, why don't I
sweep the floor. Shortly, the apprentice devil
was working as hard as the owner himself
as he waited for him to listen to his pitch
about toast landing jelly-side-up and
never hitting a red light. And whenever
the devil got impatient, the owner would say,
I'm only happy when reading Keats, or,

I've left my kidneys to a research hospital,
and the devil would imagine a great red soul
trembling like a cubic meter of raspberry Jell-O.

But it's not enough simply to crave the soul
of another creature, you have to cheat, steal,
and be generally uncivil, at which the apprentice
devil had clearly failed, and so after a week
of cooking and waiting on tables, a tall fellow
in a black cape showed up, grabbed the devil
by the scruff of the neck and dragged him off
to hell. Instead of buying a soul, he had forfeited
his own and after a brief ceremony his horns were
clipped, tail snipped, and he was kicked back up
the stairs to heaven: once an inadequate angel,
always an inadequate angel. The owner, of course,
found it a great relief to have the devil gone.
Now he could return to beating his wife while
getting ready to sell his soul for something
really big, say, a rent-controlled apartment.
What is a soul's value anyway? If the body
is made up of three dollars' worth of elements,
is the soul worth a bit more or a bit less?
Apparently, the apprentice devil's only mistake
was to go out searching in the first place
when all he needed was to open a store
and hang out a sign: Souls Bought Here.
Then think of the eager line of people
extending block after block. How could they
stand the suspense? He might not buy them all.
So ruffians would push to the front and people
start to shove. In no time, the whole street
would erupt in violence, a pitched battle—
soul cut throat, soul ball break, soul eye gouge.

AMAZING STORY

Disease of the spirit, disease of the mind—
a man is bored, terribly bored. All day
he works at a gravel pit separating
white stones from black stones. There are too many
white stones. The man feels ready to explode.
Here a stone, there a stone. One day a kid
rips by on a motorcycle, hits a patch
of oil and flips over right at the man's feet.
The kid is pretty badly smashed. He groans
and rolls around on the ground. He's in
great pain. No one else saw the accident.
The man starts to call an ambulance, then
stops to watch the kid a little longer,
moaning and twisting on the ground. You see,
he was so bored. Help me, says the kid.
In a minute, says the man. He thinks, Here
is a real life-and-death struggle. The kid
is bleeding from a hundred places. The man
has never seen a movie half so interesting.
He drags the kid off the road and goes back
to separating the stones. In just a moment
I'll call an ambulance, he thinks. But he can't
bring himself to do it. This is the real stuff,
he thinks, this is what life is all about.
Time flies. In the evening after work, the man
drags the kid to his house in a wagon.
His wife is shocked. You brute, she says, he's
almost dead. All day she's been painting her nails.
She's nearly crazy with boredom. Don't call
the ambulance just yet, she says, let's see
what he does. They put him on a plastic sheet
on the living room floor. Both legs are broken.
His body's banged up, his face is a wreck,
and he's missing an eye. It's fascinating,
says the wife. She serves dinner and they eat

on little TV trays on either side of the kid.
All evening they watch him bleed. That night
for the first time in months they make love.
In the morning the kid is dead. Oh, damn,
says the wife, just when life was picking up.
The man sticks the kid back in the wagon
and drags him to the gravel pit. He tries
to think of all the interesting things
you can do with a corpse. By now the kid's
stiff as a board and sits straight up in the wagon.
The man thinks and thinks. Just like in the comics,
a huge question mark forms above his head.
It looks like half a mushroom-shaped cloud.
Although facing each other, he and the kid
resemble bookends—maybe Rodin's Thinker,
maybe the monkey holding the human skull.
Between them appears the obligatory book.
Let's call it The Amazing Story of Mankind.
Who can guess its meaning? With equal
understanding, the dead kid and living man
gaze at its covers, wondering what's inside.

SELECTION PROCESS

Two angels meet on a fleecy white cloud.
They've been asked to thin out Minneapolis—
too many oldsters, too many kids, too many
folks in between. They're told it weakens the herd.
Each angel holds a bag of heavenly silver dollars—
St. Jude on one side, a question mark on the other—
and at random they flip them into the air
above the city. Each coin plunges downward,
gathering speed, and sometimes hits someone.
Bam! this one's dead. Bam! that one's dead.
Got one! shouts one angel. Missed! cries the other.

In a funeral home, a young woman kneels
beside the ornate coffin of her father.
But why him? she cries, he was so young.
Truly, he was taken before his time.
Meanwhile, the father waits in a huge line
before the gates of heaven. Everybody's nervous,
rustling their papers and trying to count up
all the beggars they ever gave a dime to.
How do you think they decide these things?
asks the father. My talents were needed,
says his neighbor, who in life played
third base for a Triple-A team in the south.
Just then word came down from the halo factory:
No more hiring; we've filled the third shift.
In heaven, the unemployed sit around on benches,
discussing imperfections in the perfect weather,
while in hell two demons string their bows and
prepare to fire into the overcrowded clouds above.
In this manner is hell, like heaven, populated,
meaning its citizens are not so wicked, just unlucky.

Now, to be completely fair, there should be
a third scene in which human beings drop pebbles

down some rat hole to hell, hit a few stray demons
and in such a way are we brought to this earth.
But that's not how it happens. Think of a fellow
getting off a train in a foreign city—
doesn't know the language or the money,
doesn't know the jokes. Still, he is hopeful
and stands on the platform with a silly smile
on his face. The sort of smile that says:
I may be ignorant but I'm ready to learn.
And so he is. No one is more eager
than the child first sprung into this world.
Therefore, he waits with this big smile,
ready to take his chances, take what comes,
take on the whole shebang, when, pow, a small
coin plunges out of the sky and suddenly
he has all of eternity before him.

CREEPING INTELLIGENCE

Two men take three party girls to a motel.
All night long they imitate the shapes
of a dozen different kinds of pretzels.
In the morning, one man has a crick in his back.
He can't straighten up. Goodbye, goodbye,
say the girls. His friend goes off to work.
The man still can't straighten up. He had been
well over six feet tall and now he's bent down
to little more than a yard. The whole world
looks different. He hobbles along the street
staring into people's stomachs, eye to eye
with big dogs, at chin level with the hood
ornaments of expensive cars. This was a man
who knew all the answers, who could lecture
nonstop about bald spots and eyebrows.
Now he stares up into men's beards. Breasts
loom heavily above him. What a fool I was,
he cries. Humility slaps him across the face.
He decides he must tell people of his new view
of the world so he drags a soapbox to the park
and climbs up on top. A crowd gathers.
Immediately he is again over six feet tall.
A sea of bald spots spreads beneath him.
He forgets what he wanted to say, something
about the sin of pride. People clap their hands.
The man sings every Stephen Foster song
he can remember. Then he does a little dance.
The crowd continues to clap. The man grows
so excited that he falls off the soapbox.
When he gets to his feet, he finds he can
again straighten up. Whew, what a close call.
No more party girls for him. He goes home
to his wife. Domestic bliss. In the evening
they sit before the fire and his wife knits.
The man stares at the flames and feels he has forgotten

something important. Clunk, clunk, goes his brain.
The man busts half his gray cells before he stops.
Why bother? he thinks: Life is hard enough.
Later he slaps his wife on the rump. Come on,
old horse, time for another turn in the saddle.
They go to bed. In the very act of making love,
the man has a vision of himself in a space capsule
orbiting the earth. Through the little window
he can see other capsules with other people
but they can't talk, they can only wave. They get
gradually smaller until they shrink down
to black spots on a black horizon and the man
is alone staring into the infinite night.
Then he has his orgasm and pulls out.
Goodbye, goodbye, he says to the darkness.
You know, he tells his wife, somehow it's sad.
But he can't decide what's sad or why or for how long,
or how to break free of the riddle he inhabits.
Sometimes it happens like this. Knocked off his feet
by midnight depression. He's been working too hard.
He must push aside these nagging worries. Luckily,
he knows a couple of girls. He'll invite them
to a motel—night of sexual abandon. Party girls,
where would the world be without party girls?
Time's passing, he thinks, you only live once.

WHITE PIG

A family decides to have a party.
It is a graduation or birthday.
The father buys a little white pig,
just enough for his wife and six kids
with something left over for someone special.
The father has no idea how to kill a pig
but he meets a man in a bar who says,
Don't worry, I have killed hundreds of pigs.
He is a young man with a big smile.
On the day of the party, the young man arrives
early in the morning. I have no knife,
he says. And he takes the bread knife
and begins sharpening it on a stone.
He sharpens the knife and drinks brandy.
The white pig trots through the house.
The children have tied a blue ribbon
around her neck and the baby's blue bonnet
on her head. The pig thinks she is very cute.
She lets the children feed her cookies and
ride on her back. The man with the smile keeps
sharpening and drinking, sharpening and drinking.
The morning is getting late. Why don't you
do something? says the father. The pig pokes
her head around the door, then scampers away.
The young man drinks more brandy. It is nearly noon.
Why don't you kill the pig? says the father.
He wants to get it over with. The young man
looks sullenly at the floor, looks sullenly
at the father and his neat little house.
He gets to his feet and sways back and forth.
You're drunk, says the father. The young man
raises the knife. Not too drunk to kill a pig,
he shouts. He stumbles out of the kitchen.
Where's that bitch of a pig? he shouts.
The pig is upstairs with the children.

I'm ready, says the young man, now I'm
really ready. He rushes up the stairs
and into the room where the pig is playing.
You whore! he shouts. He dives at the pig
and stabs her in the leg. The pig squeals.
Outside, shouts the father, you have to kill her
outside! The pig is terrified and rushes
around the room squealing and bleeding on the rug.
The blue bonnet slips down over one eye.
You slut! shouts the young man. He leaps
at the pig and stabs her in the shoulder.
The children are screaming. The father is shouting.
The young man chases the pig through the whole house.
You whore, you slut, you little Jew of a pig!
Outside, outside! shouts the father. He knows
the rules, knows how a pig should be killed.
For the pig, it's a nightmare. The blue bonnet
has slipped down over both eyes and she can
hardly see. She squeals over and over. There is
no sound in the world like that one.
It's a sound like hot grease in your face.
At last the young man traps the pig
in the laundry room. He leaps on her.
You black bitch of a pig! he shouts. He stabs
the pig over and over. The children
stand in the doorway crying. The father
is crying. His wife hides in the bedroom.
What a great party this has turned out to be.
Finally the pig is dead. The young man
holds her up by the hind legs. Again he is
smiling. This is one dead pig! he shouts.
He has probably stabbed her over two hundred times.
The pig looks like a piece of Swiss cheese.
The young man carries the pig to the kitchen
and begins to butcher her, then he helps

to cook the pig. All afternoon the house
is full of wonderful smells. The children
hide in their bedrooms. The mother and father
scrub and scrub to clean up the blood. At last
the pig is ready to be eaten. It is a party,
maybe a graduation or birthday.
The children refuse to come downstairs.
The mother and father don't feel hungry.
The young man sits at the table by himself.
He is served by a neighborhood girl hired
to wash the dishes. He eats and eats. Tasty,
he says, there's nothing so tasty as young pig.
He drinks wine and laughs. He stuffs himself
on the sweet flesh of the little white pig.
Late at night he is still eating. The children
are in bed, the parents are in bed. The father
lies on his back and listens to the young man singing—
hunting songs, marching songs, songs of journeys
through dark places, songs of conquest and revenge.

WRONG GODS

At the party after the poetry reading,
my stepdaughter's best trick is to fall downstairs.
She is four and can slide down head or feet first,
back or belly. We play as we can. My trick,
not being a gracious man, is to act the host.
In the hall, a woman who cares for nothing
plays at being charming, while in the kitchen
a man wants us to think his thoughts about books
have some meaning. In a briefcase by the door
is the book of poems of the woman who read.
In one she said, "All my life I have worshiped
the wrong gods." Tonight at our party we greet
the gods of arrogance, falsehood, and conceit.
Taking our turns before them, we make our bows
and kiss their hands. Why must we decrease ourselves?
At least my stepdaughter still feels delight
when she risks breaking her neck, a shrill laughter
transfixing the rest of us, attempting tricks
with nothing gambled and no trace of pleasure.

CECIL

How calm is the spring evening, and the water
barely a ripple. My son stands at the edge
tossing in pebbles, then jumping back. He knows
that someplace out there lies Europe, and he points
to an island to ask if it is France. Here
on this beach my neighbor died, a foolish man.
He had fought with his daughter, his only child,
about her boyfriend and came here to cool off
when his heart stopped. Another neighbor found him
and thought him asleep, so relaxed did he seem.
He had helped me with my house, gave me advice
on painting, plastering. For this I thank him.
As I worked, we discussed our plans, how he wished
his daughter to go to the best schools, become
a scientist or engineer. I said how
I meant to settle down and make my life here—
My son asks me about the tide, why the water
doesn't keep coming up the street to wipe out
the house where he lives alone with his mother.
Is he scared, should I console him? Should I say
that if I controlled the tide I would destroy
that house for certain? Our plans came to nothing
and now, a year later, I'm just a visitor
in my son's life. We walk down to the water,
pause, and look out at the world. How big is it?
he asks me. Bigger every day, I answer.

PURSUIT

Each thing I do I rush through so I can do
something else. In such a way do the days pass—
a blend of stock car racing and the never
ending building of a gothic cathedral.
Through the windows of my speeding car, I see
all that I love falling away: books unread,
jokes untold, landscapes unvisited. And why?
What treasure do I expect in my future?
Rather it is the confusion of childhood
loping behind me, the chaos in the mind,
the failure chipping away at each success.
Glancing over my shoulder I see its shape
and so move forward, as someone in the woods
at night might hear the sound of approaching feet
and stop to listen; then, instead of silence
he hears some creature trying to be silent.
What else can he do but run? Rushing blindly
down the path, stumbling, struck in the face by sticks;
the other ever closer, yet not really
hurrying or out of breath, teasing its kill.

THE PARTY

You enter a room—Indians, Iraqis,
Indonesians, and at the kitchen table
a woman in a white blouse. You talk to her.
The host is a poet from Peru. His guests
are writers except for this woman, who studies
biology. For some reason you never
remember, you talk to her about reality
and imagination in the poetry
of Wallace Stevens. At one point you feel like
reaching out, touching your fingers to her cheek,
and this surprises you so much that you pull back.
This is your wife, the woman you finally marry.
One night years later you stare at the long cut
in her belly, out of which your only child
was brought into this world. You two, man and wife,
have had much trouble—a life like sandpaper
against the skin—and the cut in her belly
is like a symbol of all that has happened,
as if your heart or hers was torn from that spot.
Yet often, seeing her, you still desire
to reach out, lay your fingers against her cheek.
You remember in Stevens the words "Let be
be finale of seem." You told her this meant
that what exists is more important than what
seems to exist. The scar on your wife's belly
resembles six inches of comic book lightning,
sometimes it strikes one way, sometimes another.
Always it is such a confusion, trying
to know what is real and what imagined.
The party was shortly after Thanksgiving.
The year had begun badly, then got better,
to become a time when life seemed easy.
Even the weather stayed mild, with marigolds
outside the door until into December.
Then the whole mess began to tilt. Light to dark,

you feel pushed from light to dark. Often it seems
the wish to touch her cheek is the one reason
you stay together, that stubborn desire
that gets left over when all the rest collapses.

ODYSSEUS'S HOMECOMING

You see, it was the deception that did it,
the lies; there was no one Odysseus couldn't deceive,
including himself. The greatest liar in the world,
Athena had said. How else could he have thought
twenty years were nothing, that all had stayed
the same? It had become such a confusion—
the stories he had told the world and himself—
so much so that when he approached his palace
dressed as a beggar he nearly wept to see it existed.
This is my home, he thought, not knowing the word.
This is my son, he thought, not recognizing him.
So although he knew his palace, knew even his old dog,
he kept silent. Why does it look so different?
he wondered. Perhaps even Troy was a story and Circe
and his men changed to pigs, and the sirens—
he couldn't keep it straight in his head. And so
he was confused and polite to the suitors, all
one hundred and twelve, and thought there might be
some error and withheld his anger. Twenty years,
he asked, are you sure he's been gone twenty years?
And the suitors mocked him as an ignorant old man
and refused to give him scraps from the table.
Is this really my table? he asked himself. He saw
how the suitors ate and drank his wine, laughed
and amused themselves with his servant girls.
Are these my servants? asked Odysseus, did I ever
live here, and if I lived here, why did I leave?
It was seeing Penelope that brought it back.
He had kept her picture in his mind, a girl
just twenty—how lovely she had looked with
her dark hair and skin the color of fresh cream.
When he was brought before her, she didn't know him.
Is this her? he asked himself. It was not that
she was ugly or much changed but only that she was
twenty years older and there was gray in her hair
and her face was lined. Is this Penelope?

But he knew she was Penelope, knew this had been
his life, recognized his son, his servants, his home.
He looked around him and all his stories fell away.
What a fool I was, he thought, see what I have lost.
He saw her indifference, the deadness in her eyes.
She was no more than a creature who had waited
for a bright time and now that time had gone by,
as a flower goes by, or a fruit, or a season,
and here he was returned to claim his winter wife.
Of course he grew angry, that was his nature.
He slapped and struck at himself with his knife,
but it wasn't enough. The suitors mocked him.
They had come expecting to marry his widow and
they laughed at him. What could he do but kill them?
Taking his bow, he shot one through the throat,
put an arrow through the liver of another. How
they fled, like termites fleeing from a fire.
How they piled up at the locked doors. He killed
all one hundred and twelve, killed their supporters
and servants, killed even their horses. And always
in his mind was the picture of Penelope, how she
had looked standing by the shore in her white robes
as he sailed off to Troy. He had no lies left.
He tried to tell himself there were other girls,
that he could father more sons, but there was no
deception that could hide him. So he brought out
the twelve serving girls who had slept and amused
themselves with the suitors and had them clean the blood
from the walls and floors. How pretty they looked
with their black hair and pale skin. But Odysseus
had no place in his heart for their beauty, no lie
where they could settle and stay young in his mind.
So he hung them, strung them up in the great hall.
How they kicked up their feet to the music
of his anger—twelve pretty maids all in a row.

THE GRAVEDIGGER'S PLEASURE

Sometimes it comes down to very little: a man
in a coffee shop spending his afternoons
at a table in a corner. He is the opposite
of deaf—when he speaks, no one listens.
How cold it is, he says, for this time of year.
He has never known the dark to come so fast.
At night on the beach, he watches an ocean liner
steam out of the harbor, a dark thing encrusted
with light. From across the water, he listens
to the ship's band playing some of the songs
he once danced to, until it seems he can hear
the rustle of his wife's taffeta dress. Later,
he leans against the church wall, arguing not
exactly with the ghost of his wife but maybe
with the idea of her—he tells her how she was
a terrible cook, how the house was always dirty.
But none of that matters now. Why has she
deserted him? Still later, he stands on a hill
as wind flicks the gray strands of his hair.
He thinks of the stars, the other solar systems
he knows nothing about and if people live there,
what their dreams are and what makes them sad.
When he doesn't show up at the cafe, it takes
the waitresses a week to notice. Maybe he went
south, says one, you know, to avoid the cold.
She tries to think if he drank his coffee black
or with milk, if his hands had lain still
or flipped back and forth on the counter,
but then she forgets and he slips from her mind
as one might drop a paper sack down a chute.
At the whorehouse, the gravedigger has money.
He feels full of himself and waits his turn.
He likes to make the fat one squat down
on all fours, then mount her from behind.

OLD HOUSE

So much death in the room but no people—
the candles burned down to their stumps,
the food untouched, the meat growing cold
in its grease. Under the couch, the cat plays
with a mole it dragged in from the barn.
The mole crawls off. The cat drags it back.
If cats could laugh, this one would be laughing.
The air in the room is thick with shouting,
although no words are left. The woman is upstairs
trying to write a letter. The man is outside
measuring the dead space between the stars.
The air is thick the way cold gravy is thick,
the way air in a dream is thick when you run
and whatever is pursuing you gets closer.
The only sound comes from the stereo, where
the needle is stuck at the end of the record.
Click, click, it says, click, click—a sound
like the detritus of all their words together.
They are not here to listen. She is upstairs,
jabbing her pen repeatedly against paper.
He is outside staring up at the holes in the sky.
How sloppy the sky looks with light leaking from it
like water from a cracked ceiling. But what
can he do about it? He has no wish to fix it,
nor is he yet brave enough to drag it down.

THE NIHILIST

He was depressed so he made something.
He created light but it made nothing better.
It burned his face; it hurt his eyes.
So he made water to soothe and refresh him
and the light flickered on miles of blue water
but it wasn't enough. I'm tired, he said,
I need a place to sit. So he made earth.
The light is too bright, he said, I need shade.
So he made trees. I need something beautiful,
he said. So he made the moon and stars, and saw
how they glittered and filled the night sky,
but they made nothing better. I'm bored, he said,
I need toys. So he made birds and every kind
of creeping thing. I need servants, he said,
creatures to do as I tell them. So he made
men and women and watched them scurry across
the earth eager to please him and do his bidding.
But their desires bored him, they filled him
with exhaustion. I'll make them move faster,
he said. So he gave them discontent and hunger.
Then he set Death as his captain over them
and watched them march around on the earth
until he wanted to laugh and slap his knee
but it wasn't enough, the vacancy stayed within him.
He looked at what he had made—the light and water,
the little human creatures. What a mess it was,
what a complication of celestial doodling.
And to the desperate, those with the biggest appetite,
he said, You can keep it, you can do with it
what you will. Then he lifted himself up to the stars,
those baubles of light, and gently he set his face
among them so it shown forth with its teeth
and dark eyes, its vast brow of discontent.
Then he began to scrape and rub at it
so that his greatest creation would be his own

obliteration, and his face blinked out like a dying spark,
leaving the human creatures running back and forth,
craning their necks and calling out the many names
they had given him, although he still hung there
had anyone the ability to see him. That's his face,
that vacancy between the stars, that dark place
filling the sky as water fills a cup, or a room
without people, no tables or chairs or pictures
on the walls. This is an empty room, you say.
Wrong, wrong again. Listen carefully, hear the laughter.

CEMETERY NIGHTS IV

Betting on how many leaves cover a birch,
then counting them. Betting how many Buicks
drive by the graveyard in a single week,
then doing the sums. Betting how many crows fly
north–south as opposed to east–west in a single month,
then adding them up. Such are the games of the dead.
Holidays, with their burden of memories,
are even worse. Christmas, Easter, George
Washington's Birthday, even Halloween
is a time for weeping and the gnashing
of those few remaining teeth. One Thanksgiving
a turkey fell from the back of a speeding truck,
staggered into the graveyard and collapsed.
The dead stood round and watched. When the turkey
revived, it had eyes only for the maggots which
the dead wear as a socialite wears her jewels.
For a turkey, maggots mean feasting and pleasure, which
is the difference between a living and dead
Thanksgiving. In life, a dozen friends surround
one dead bird. In death, one living turkey attempts
to round up a dozen dead. . . . Were they friends?
No, in death there are only acquaintances.

Luckily, a young man was hurrying by and he
saw the turkey, grabbed it, and wrung its neck.
How simple are these problems for the living.
He was on his way to his parents for dinner.
They were poor. It was the old story. No
turkey for them, maybe hamburger or chicken.
Now all was changed. He would toss the turkey
down on the table and his father would grin,
in that way he used to, and reach out and very
lightly he would tap his son's jaw with his fist.
As the son hurried toward this certain pleasure,
he thought of how his father used to carry him

up to bed, the rough feel of his father's bristles
against his cheek and the smell of hair oil
and sweat. How long ago that seemed. What train
was carrying him such a distance from that time,
and what dark fields would be his destination?

ON THE FAMOUS PAINTING
BY ROUSSEAU

There was a fellow who made himself a bird suit;
I remember seeing pictures. The plan was to jump
off the Eiffel Tower and fly a bit over the roofs
of Paris, surprising the artists sitting at tables
at outdoor cafes discussing the various Isms—
because this was long ago and in the picture
the dignitaries wear top hats as they gather to watch
this bird man put the artists to shame. Look
at this fabulous bird suit, both beautiful and
functional, an example of life improving on art.
Of course, the poor fellow fell like a rock—
snapshots of pathetic fluttering and astounded
top hats. You wonder what the inventor thought
as he plummeted past the elevator going down.
Was he still optimistic, muttering, Just a little
tinkering and a few more owl feathers on the wing?
Then a picture of the dignitaries looking rather
birdlike themselves as they gather around this
dark mound of feathers on the ground. There had been
a bump, a dismal thud, just enough to disturb
the painter from his reverie and send him back
to stare at his canvas. This was before the turn
of the century so let's say the painter was Rousseau,
a kindly man who collected tolls for a living,
and he is just raising his brush to put a few
last strokes on his painting of the Sleeping Gypsy.
You know the one, where the gypsy in his coat
of many colors is sleeping on the desert sand
while right behind him a lion is snuffling what
is probably the last of the gypsy's evening meal.
The question is whether the gypsy is sleeping or just
pretending and is actually scared stiff, thinking,
Don't bite me, don't bite me, don't bite me.
At least this is what the dignitaries think when
they happen to see the picture in one of the salons

and this is what we've been thinking ever since,
which makes the picture a good warning not to sleep
in open places, a work of art both functional and
beautiful, designed to be hung in state parks where
there are certain ruffians amongst the wild life.
But Rousseau—in those moments after the bird man
took his plunge and was muttering to himself, Maybe
I stepped off on the wrong foot—Rousseau raised
his brush and tinkered with the grin on the face
of the moon, added a bit of white to the gypsy's
eyes and teeth, as if he might be awake, alert but
terrified, painted the highlights on the gypsy's jug
and primitive guitar to show he was a man who liked
good times and was no better than he ought to be,
like anyone in fact. As for the question of exactly
what he knew, Rousseau left that in doubt, for what
do we ever know about the next moment, no matter
what we hope or have carefully planned? No sir,
the park guards had told the sleeping gypsy,
there are no lions in this desert, not a one.
Just like the bird man perched on a railing
of the Eiffel Tower and he thinking of a range
of possibility and all of it benign, and yet he
dropped like a rock, a dumb idea, something
already dead, muttering as he fell to earth:
Chalk one up for reckless pride, the wages
of hubris are darkness, desolation, and despair.

PRIME MOVER

Two bums sit on a park bench discussing
the price of beans when suddenly there appears
before them a small pink cloud, out of which pops
a cherubic hand, fingers like sausages and pudgy
at the wrist. The hand gives each bum a gold brick
then disappears to the notes of celestial music.
Needless to say, the bums are thrown for a loop
and gape at the treasure smack in their laps
until each turns his attention to the gold brick
in his buddy's lap, which seems bigger and
gives forth a brighter shine. Within seconds,
they begin to fight and shortly one of the bums
runs off with both bricks tucked beneath his arm.
Time passes. His situation improves. But then
he meets another man with two gold bricks and each,
who had been satisfied, sees his own treasure
lose its gleam and so they fight and soon
the proud winner trots off with all four bricks.
Needless to say, he soon meets another with four
gold bricks and each feels dissatisfied so they too
fight, and the winner with eight bricks meets another
and they fight, then the winner with sixteen bricks
meets another, and the situation repeats and repeats
until we reach a man with a million gold bricks
which he keeps walled up in a mountain. No more
fooling around, he thinks, no more funny stuff.
And when further gold bricks arrive, he just drops
them down a chute where they clang-bang on top
of his treasure, which in fact he never sees.
But this is not the end of the cherubic hand, because
often it is parked on the other side of the mountain,
where it can easily scrape down through the rocks
and dirt, dig into the hoard of gold and extract
a pair of gold bricks, then whiz up into the sky.
On the nearby branch of a blasted oak, a sparrow

wonders, just what kind of hand is this anyway—
celestial, bestial, comical, or run-of-the-mill?
Why not ask the two bums riding a freight car
between Sioux City and Des Moines, ask them
the nature of the hand that appears from nowhere
to give them each a glittering gold brick, then
flits off to perform figure eights above the boxcars.
On another track, on a train headed west, a woman
from Davenport sees the flying hand and decides
it must be an angel, while a salesman from Waterloo
thinks it a devil and pulls down his shade. But
the conductor, who is widely traveled, wonders
if this isn't the force of life itself, the force
that sometimes brings good cheer and sometimes
sadness, like the sadness one of the bums now feels
as he looks at his buddy, who has been his friend
for twenty years, yet even so he gives him a push,
snatches his brick and watches him tumble out
into the bright Iowa sunset—so golden, so final.

BOWLERS ANONYMOUS

Here comes the woman who wears the plastic prick
hooked to a string around her waist, the man who
puts girls' panties like a beanie on his head,
the chicken molester, the lady who likes great Danes,
the boy who likes sheep, the old fellow who likes
to watch turkeys dance on the top of a hot stove,
the bicycle-seat sniffer, grasshopper muncher,
the bubbles-in-the-bath biter—they all meet
each night at midnight and, oh lord, they bowl.
From twelve to six they take it out on the pins
as they discuss their foibles with their friends.
I'm trying to cut down, says the woman who nibbles
the tails of mice. I've thrown away my Zippo, says
the man who sticks matches between people's toes.
There is nothing that can't become a pleasure
if one lets it, and so they bowl. They think
of that oddly handsome German shepherd face
and they bowl. Their hands quiver at the thought
of jamming their fingers in a car door
and they bowl. These are the heroes, these
grocers and teachers and postmen and plumbers.
They bring snapshots of themselves and Scotch tape,
then fix their photos to the pins and they bowl.
They focus on their faces at the end of the alley
and they bowl. They see the hunger in their eyes,
the twist of anticipation in their lips, and oh
they bowl—bowl and remember, bowl and forget,
as the pins with their own bruised faces explode
from midnight to six. While in those explosions
of wood, in which each pin describes an exact arc,
they feast on those brief moments when something
becomes perfect—like a curled wave, Beethoven
quartet, or the wind hitting a dandelion clock—
one of those moments when the world seems to stop

and everything conspires to push some fleeting
beauty—ripening peach or blossoming rose—
to the queer brink of perfection, where it flames,
flickers, fades, and is never perfect again.

SHORT RIDES

What is the division between good intention
and best behavior? Or rather, let's say it's
a fence, a ditch, some sort of barrier, since
many times we stand on one side looking over
at the creature we should be but aren't. And this,
it seems, is where we are often most human,
lost in the country between Want To and Can't.

A man is hitchhiking. The devil picks him up.
Where to? says the devil, who is in disguise
and looks like an old lady in a blue straw hat
who just happens to be driving a Ferrari.
My father is sick, I must see him, says
the man, who's never been in a Ferrari before.
This one is red and very fast. The world
flies by. Apparently by accident, they zoom past
the father's house. The man doesn't speak.
After a few more blocks, the devil makes
a U-turn and drives him back. That was
a real treat, says the man. Inside, he finds
that two weeks have gone by. His father
is dead and buried. Everyone is disappointed.
Even the police have been out looking. What
can I say, says the man, I guess I let you down.
The phone rings. It's his wife, who tells him,
Come home right away. The man hitchhikes home.
The devil picks him up in his bright red Ferrari.
By now the man is suspicious but as they
whiz by his house he doesn't make a peep.
He leans back and feels the sun on his brow.
When the devil gets him home, two more weeks
have disappeared. His wife has moved out lock,
stock, and barrel; the house is empty except
for the telephone, which begins to ring. Now
it's his mother who's sick. I'll be right over,

says the man. The Ferrari is waiting at the curb.
The man doesn't hesitate. He leaps inside.
He leans back. Once more the wind is in his hair.
He wallows in soft leather as in a warm bath.
But this time he knows the score, knows the driver
isn't a little old lady, knows they will zoom
past his mother's house, that he won't protest.
He knows his mother will die, that he'll miss
the funeral. He searches his soul for just
a whisper of guilt, but if it's there, it's been
drowned out by the purr of the big motor.
Am I really so weak? the man asks himself.
And he peers across that metaphorical ditch
to the sort of person he would like to be,
but he can't make the jump, bridge the gap.
Why can't I fight off temptation? he asks.
He sees his future is as clear as a map
with all the bad times circled in red.
He knows that as crisis is piled on crisis
He will find the Ferrari waiting at the curb,
and that no matter how hard he tries to resist
he will succumb at last to the wish to feel
the wind riffle his hair, the touch of leather,
to be lulled by the gentle vibration of the motor
as life slips by in a succession of short rides.

THE NOISE THE HAIRLESS MAKE

How difficult to be an angel.
In order to forgive, they have no memory.
In order to be good, they're always forgetting.
How else could heaven be run? Still,
it needs to be full of teachers and textbooks
imported from God's own basement, since only
in hell is memory exact. In one classroom,
a dozen angels scratch their heads as their teacher
displays the cross-section of a human skull,
saying, Here is the sadness, here
the anger, here's where laughter is kept.
And the angels think, How strange, and take notes
and would temper their forgiveness if it weren't
all forgotten by the afternoon. Sometimes
a bunch fly down to earth with their teacher,
who wants them to study a living example, and
this evening they find a man lying in a doorway
in an alley in Detroit. They stand around
chewing their pencils as their teacher says,
This is the stick he uses to beat his wife,
this is the bottle he drinks from when he
wants to forget, this is the Detroit Tigers
T-shirt he wears whenever he's sad, this is
the electric kazoo he plays in order to weep.
And the angels think, How peculiar, and wonder
whether to temper their forgiveness or just
let it ride, which really doesn't matter since
they forget the question as soon as it's asked.
But their muttering wakes the man in the doorway,
who looks to see a flock of doves departing
over the trash cans. And because he dreamed
of betrayal and pursuit, of defeat in battle,
the death of friends, he heaves a bottle at them
and it breaks under a streetlight so the light
reflects on its hundred broken pieces with such

a multicolored twinkling that the man laughs.
From their place on a brick wall, the angels
watch and one asks, What good are they? Then
others take up the cry, What good are they,
what good are they? But as fast as they articulate
the question it's forgotten and their teacher,
a minor demon, returns with them to heaven.
But the man, still chuckling, sits in his doorway,
and the rats in their dumpsters hear this sound
like stones rattling or metal banging together,
and they see how the man is by himself without
food or companions, without work or family
or a real bed for his body. They creep back
to their holes and practice little laughs
that sound like coughing or a dog throwing up
as once more they uselessly try to imitate
the noise the hairless make when defeated.

WARNING

Like a living thing, the November wind struck
and struck against his house so the windows shook
and bed quaked until deep in the night he thought
his home would tumble down into the ocean.
Going to the window, he saw three women
gathering sticks on his front lawn, hunched over
as they looped back and forth through the winter grass,
tucking sticks in the pockets of their aprons.
The man stood back to hide himself. He imagined
their bright eyes like searchlights raking across
the blue flannel of his winter pajamas.
Later he slept. When he woke, he told himself
the women were a dream. It had snowed in the night,
but now the sky was clear. Looking at the snow,
he saw a crimson speck which he later found
was the single red wing of a cardinal,
no body or other feathers, no footprints,
and this terrified him—just the single wing
lying like a bookmark on the snow's white page,
as if the three women were reminding him
of their constant place in his life and that time
when they will come at last to lead him away.
Some days he stares out at the ocean and sees
the water and sky as a picture, a Chinese
painting with boats and water and blue sky.
He hates the certainty of his mortality,
the fragility of tissue that sustains him.
All through each day no matter where he is,
part of him waits at the window for the picture
to be torn asunder, waits for the great hand
to burst through and drag him to oblivion.

SUN GAZERS

My stepdaughter is three and we have some games
we play when she gets back from day care and I
have finished my work for the day. In one game,
while I try to find her she climbs on a chair
and closes her eyes because with her eyes shut
she thinks I can't see her but must prowl around
calling her name, which I do to amuse her.
Then tiptoeing back I give her a slight poke,
which pleases her as proof of my cleverness,
that I've found her secret place in all that dark.
The mind too, I think, has many eyes, which we
open one by one, as if the world's too bright,
as waking at night and turning on the lamp
I keep an eye squinched shut and feel unprepared
to face the glare. My stepdaughter with eyes shut
feels safe as I circle her dark hiding place—
to look around her means perceiving danger,
yet soon she will come to look into the light.
Death too is a kind of light, a larger sun
we spend our lives learning to look into
as if by seeing we might defeat our end,
like those Indian holy men who live by
staring at the sun, trying to discover
what lies past common sight, and so die blind.

WAKING

Waking, I look at you sleeping beside me.
It is early and the baby in her crib
has begun her conversation with the gods
that direct her, cooing and making small hoots.
Watching you, I see how your face bears the signs
of our time together—for each objective
description, there is the romantic; for each
scientific fact, there's the subjective truth—
this line is from days spent at a microscope,
this from when you thought I no longer loved you.
Last night a friend called to say that he intends
to move out; so simple, he and his wife splitting
like a cell into two separate creatures.
What would happen if we divided ourselves?
As two colors blend on a white pad, so we
have become a third color; or better,
as a wire bites into the tree it surrounds,
so we have grown together. Can you believe
how frightening I find this, to know I have
no life except with you? It's almost enough
to make me destroy it just to protest it.
Always we seemed perched on the brink of chaos.
But today there's just sunlight and the baby's
chatter, her wonder at the way light dances
on the wall. How lucky to be ignorant,
to greet joy without a trace of suspicion,
to take that first step without worrying what
comes trailing after, as night trails after day,
or winter summer, or confusion where all
seemed clear and each moment was its own reward.

STREETLIGHT

The streetlight from my parents' bed at night split
so perfectly into four branches of light
that at five I knew one could surely be climbed.
Lying in their bed, I pictured myself perched
on that crossbar of radiance, ready to
shinny up its cold flame to discover what?
That was the question, what happened at the top?
Again it seemed I had found another door
out of this world, another way to vanish.
But at five what was this need to disappear?—
as if I could creep under the bright curtain
of landscape to find out what the darkness was
or escape into a place from children's books,
a place important for being someplace else.
I think about that childhood self, so distant,
so foreign to any feeling that I have
it's as if he really broke free and might now
be wandering through some city, one of those kids
you pass on the street, who looks into your eyes,
as if to say, I know you, I despise you,
you're nothing I desire—then looks away.

THESEUS WITHIN THE LABYRINTH

For Stratis Haviaras

The lives of Greeks in the old days were deep,
mysterious, and often lead to questions like,
Just what was wrong with Ariadne anyway, that's
what I'd like to know? She would have done
anything for that rascally Theseus, and what
did he do but sneak out in the night and row
back to his ship with black sails. Let's get
the heck out of here, he muttered to his crew,
and they leaned on their oars as he went whack-
whack on the whacking block—a human metronome
of adventure and ill-fortune. She was King Minos's
daughter and had helped Theseus kill the king's
pet monster, her half brother, so possibly
he didn't like feeling beholden—people might
think he wasn't tough. But certainly he'd spent
his life knocking chips off shoulders and flattening
any fellow reckless enough to step across a line
drawn in the dust. If you wanted a punch thrown,
Theseus was just the cowboy to throw it. I'm only
happy when hitting and scratching, he'd told Ariadne
that first night. So he'd been the logical choice
to sail down from Athens to Crete to stop this
nonsense of a tribute of virgins for some
monster to eat. Those Cretans called it eating but
Theseus thought himself no fool and liked a virgin
as well as the next man. Not that he could have got
into the labyrinth without Ariadne's help, or out
either for that matter. As for the Minotaur, lounging
on his couch, nibbling grapes and sipping wine while
a troop of ex-virgins fluttered to his beck and call,
Theseus must have scared the horns right off him,
slamming back the door and standing there in his lion
skin suit and waving that ugly club. The poor beast
might have had a stroke had there been time before
Theseus pummeled him into the earth. Then, with

Ariadne's help, Theseus escaped, and soon after he
ditched her on an island and sailed off in his ship
with black sails, which returns us to the question:
Just what was wrong with Ariadne anyway?
But nobody like Theseus likes a smart girl, always
telling him to dress warmly and eat plenty of fiber.
She was one of those people who are never in doubt.
Had he sharpened his sword, tied his sandals?
Without her, of course, he would have never escaped
the labyrinth. Why hadn't he thought of that trick
with the ball of yarn? But as he looked down
at her sleeping form, this woman who was already
carrying his child, maybe he thought of their
future together, how she would correctly foretell
the mystery or banality behind each locked door.
So probably he shook his head and said, Give me
a dumb girl any day, and crept back to his ship
and sailed away. Of course Ariadne was revenged.
She would have told him to change the sails,
to take down the black ones, put up the white.
She would have reminded him that his father,
the king of Athens, was waiting on a high cliff
scanning the Aegean for Theseus's returning ship,
white for victory, black for defeat. She would
have said how his father would see the black sails,
how the grief for the supposed death of his one son
would destroy him. But Theseus and his men had
brought out the wine and were cruising a calm sea
in a small boat filled to the brim with ex-virgins.
Who could have blamed him? Until he heard the distant
scream and his head shot up to see the black sails
and he knew. The girls disappeared, the ship grew
quiet except for the lap-lap of the water. Staring
toward the spot where his father had tumbled
head first into the Aegean, Theseus understood

he would always be a stupid man with a thick stick,
scratching his forehead long after the big event.
But think, does he change his mind, turn back
the ship, hunt up Ariadne, and beg her pardon?
Far better to be stupid by himself than smart
because she'd been tugging on his arm; better
to live in the eternal present with a boatload
of ex-virgins than in that dark land of consequences
promised by Ariadne, better to live like any one of us,
thinking to outwit the darkness, but knowing
it will catch us, that we will be surprised like
the Minotaur on his couch when the door slams back
and the hired gun of our personal destruction bursts
upon us, upsetting the good times and scaring the girls.
Better to be ignorant, to go into the future as into
a long tunnel, without ball of yarn or clear direction,
to tiptoe forward like any fool or saint or hero,
jumpy, full of second thoughts, and bravely unprepared.

TO PULL INTO ONESELF
AS INTO A LOCKED ROOM

These are days of sickness and forgetting.
A man stands in line at a whorehouse.
Tonight there is something special.
The other girls paint their nipples black
and spit on the men waiting in line.
The man keeps moving forward. He reaches
a room where a woman is lying on her back.
What is so special about this?
A telescope is tucked up between
her legs, tucked right up inside her.
One by one the men go to her,
kneel down between her fat white thighs.
At last it's the man's turn.
Kneeling down on a blue rug,
he leans forward between the whore's legs.
He puts his eye to the telescope.
Shortly, he sees himself as he was
years before, sees himself as a small child.
His parents are giving him a bath.
They are talking and laughing. They lift him
from the tub, dry him with warm towels.
His father carries him to the bedroom.
He snuggles down between cool white sheets.
Someone slaps him on the back. Come on,
you son of a pig, your time's up. The whore
snaps her fingers at the next in line.
The man goes downstairs to the street.
It has begun to rain, great black drops
that smash and break on the pavement.
The man has a hundred friends he could visit
but to each one he says no.

HE TOLD HER HE LOVED HER

Party all day, party all night—a man
wakes up on the floor of a friend's kitchen.
It's still dark. He can hear people snoring.
He reaches out and touches long silky hair.
He thinks it's his friend's daughter. Actually,
it's a collie dog. He can't see a thing
without his glasses. He embraces the dog.
Why is the daughter wearing a fur coat?
He gropes around for the daughter's breasts
but can't find them. The dog licks his face.
So that's how it's going to be, is it?
The man licks the collie dog back. He tries
to take off his pants but gets his underwear
caught in the zipper, so they only smooch.
He tells the collie dog about his wife,
how they only make love once a month.
He tells the collie dog about his two sons,
how they have robbed him blind and ruined
the record player. The dog licks his face.
The man tells the collie dog that he loves her.
He decides in the morning he and the daughter
will run away and immigrate to New Zealand.
They will raise sheep and children. Each evening
as the sun sets they will embrace on their
front porch with a deep sense of accomplishment.
He will stop drinking and playing cards.
The man falls asleep with the image of
the little log house clearly before his eyes.
When he wakes in the morning, he finds
the collie dog curled up beside him. You bitch,
he cries, and kicks her out of the kitchen.
He staggers off to find the daughter's bedroom.
Time to leave for New Zealand, my precious.
The daughter screams. The father comes running,
grabs his friend, and throws him out of the house.

Later the father has lunch with a priest.
He describes how this fat old clerk had tried
to rape his daughter. Was it drugs, whiskey,
or general depravity? They both wonder at
the world's approaching collapse. Sometimes
at night the father starts awake as if
he'd missed a step and was suddenly falling.
Where am I? he asks. What am I doing?
The waitress brings them coffee. The father
can't take his eyes off her. He forgets
what he was thinking. She has breasts the size
of his head. He wants to take off his shoes
and run back and forth across her naked body.
Let us leave him with his preoccupation.
Like an airborne camera, the eye of the poem
lifts and lifts until the two men are only
two dark shapes seated at the round table
of an outdoor cafe. The season is autumn.
The street is full of cars. It is cloudy.
This is the world where Socrates was born;
where Jesse James was shot in the back
as he reached up to straighten a picture;
where a fat old clerk prowls the streets,
staring into the face of every dog he meets,
seeking out the features of his own true love.

QUERENCIA

In the children's story of Ferdinand the Bull,
the bull gets off. He sits down, won't fight.
He manages to walk out of the ring without that
sharp poke of steel being shoved through
his back and deep into his heart. He returns
to the ranch and the sniffing of flowers.
But in real life, once the bull enters the ring,
then it's a certainty he will leave ignominiously,
dragged out by two mules while the attention of
the crowd rivets on the matador, who, if he's good,
holds up an ear, taken from the bull, and struts
around the ring, since it is his business to strut
as it is the bull's business to be dragged away.
. . . . .

It is the original eagerness of the bull which
takes one's breath. Suddenly he is there, hurtling
at the barrier, searching for something soft and
human to flick over his shoulder, trying to hook
his horn smack into the glittering belly
of the matador foolish enough to be there.
But there is a moment after the initial teasing
when the bull realizes that ridding the ring
of these butterfly creatures is not what
the afternoon is about. Sometimes it comes with
the first wrench of his back when the matador
turns him too quickly. Sometimes it comes
when the picador is driving his lance into
the bull's crest—the thick muscle between
the shoulder blades. Sometimes it comes when
the banderillos place their darts into that same
muscle and the bull shakes himself, trying to
free himself of that bright light in his brain.
Or it may come even later, when the matador
is trying to turn the bull again and again,
trying to wrench that same muscle which he uses

to hold up his head, to charge, to toss a horse.
It is the moment the bull stops and almost thinks,
when the eagerness disappears and the bull
realizes these butterflies can cause him pain,
when he turns to hunt out his querencia.
. . . . .

It sounds like care: querencia—and it means
affection or fondness, coming from *querer*,
to want or desire or love, but also to accept
a challenge as in a game, but also it means
a place chosen by a man or animal—querencia—
the place one cares most about, where one is
most secure, protected, where one feels safest.
In the ring, it may be a spot near the gate
or the place he was first hurt or where
the sand is wet or where there's a little blood,
his querencia, even though it looks like any
other part of the ring, except this is the spot
the bull picks as his home, the place he will
defend and keep returning to, the place where
he again decides to fight and lifts his head
despite the injured muscle, the place the matador
tries to keep him away from, where the bull,
sensing defeat, is most dangerous and stubborn.
. . . . .

The passage through adulthood is the journey
through bravado, awareness, and resignation
which the bull duplicates in his fifteen minutes
in the ring. As for the querencia, we all have
a place where we feel safest, even if it is only
the idea of a place, maybe an idea by itself,
the place that all our being radiates out from,
like an ideal of friendship or justice or perhaps
something simpler like the memory of a back porch
where we laughed a lot and how the setting sun

through the pine trees shone on the green chairs,
flickered off the ice cubes in our glasses.
We all have some spot in our mind which we
go back to from hospital bed, or fight with
husband or wife, or the wreckage of a life.
So the bull's decision is only the degree
to which he decides to fight, since the outcome
is already clear, since the mules are already
harnessed to drag his body across the sand.
Will he behave bravely and with dignity or
will he be fearful with his thick tongue lolling
from his mouth and the blood making his black
coat shiny and smooth? And the audience, no matter
how much it admires the matador, watches the bull
and tries to catch a glimpse of its own future.
· · · · ·

At the end, each has a knowledge which is just
of inevitability, so the only true decision
is how to behave, like anyone supposedly—
the matador who tries to earn the admiration
of the crowd by displaying grace and bravery
in the face of peril, the bull who can't
be said to decide but who obeys his nature.
Probably, he has no real knowledge and,
like any of us, it's pain that teaches him
to be wary, so his only desire in defeat
is to return to that spot of sand, and even
when dying he will stagger toward his querencia
as if he might feel better there, could
recover there, take back his strength, win
the fight, stick that glittering creature to the wall,
while the matador tries to weaken that one muscle—
the animal all earnestness, the man all deceit—
until they come to that instant when the matador
decides the bull is ready and the bull appears

to submit by lowering his head, where the one
offers his neck and the other offers his belly,
and the matador's one hope is for a clean kill,
that the awful blade of the horn won't suddenly
rear up into the white softness of his groin.

One October in Barcelona I remember watching
a boy, an apprentice, lunge forward for the kill
and miss and miss again, how the bull would fling
the sword out of his back and across the ring,
and again stagger to his feet and shake himself,
and how the boy would try again and miss again,
until his assistant took a dagger and stabbed
repeatedly at the spinal cord as the bull tried
to drag himself forward to that place in the sand,
that querencia, as the crowd jeered and threw
their cushions and the matador stood back ashamed.
It was cold and the sun had gone down. The brightly
harnessed mules were already in the ring, and everyone
wanted to forget it and go home. How humiliating
it seemed and how hard the bull fought at the end
to drag himself to that one spot of safety, as if
that word could have any meaning in such a world.

CEMETERY NIGHTS V

Wheel of memory, wheel of forgetting, bitter
taste in the mouth—those who have been dead longest
group together in the center of the graveyard
facing inward. The sooner they become dust the better.
They pick at their flesh and watch it crumble,
they chip at their bones and watch them dissolve.
Do they have memories? Just shadows in the mind
like a hand passing between a candle and a wall.
Those who have been dead a lesser time stand
closer to the fence, but already they have started
turning away. Maybe they still have some sadness.
And what are their thoughts? Colors mostly,
sunset, sunrise, a burning house, someone waving
from the flames. Those who have recently died
line up against the fence facing outward,
watching the mailman, deliverymen, the children
returning from school, listening to the church bells
dealing out the hours of the living day.
So arranged, the dead form a great spoked wheel—
such is the fiery wheel that rolls through heaven.

For the rats, nothing is more ridiculous
than the recently dead as they press against
the railing with their arms stuck between the bars.
Occasionally, one sees a friend, even a loved one.
Then what a shouting takes place as the dead
tries to catch the eye of the living. One actually
sees his wife waiting for a bus and he reaches out
so close that he nearly touches her yellow hair.
During life they were great lovers. Maybe
he should throw a finger at her, something
to attract her attention. Like a scarecrow
in a stiff wind, the dead husband waves his arms.
Is she aware of anything? Perhaps a slight breeze
on an otherwise still day, perhaps a smell of earth.

And what does she remember? Sometimes, when
she sits in his favorite chair or drinks a wine
that he liked, she will recall his face but
much faded, like a favorite dress washed too often.
And her husband, what does he think? As a piece
of crumpled paper burns within a fire,
so the thought of her burns within his brain.
And where is she going? These days she has taken
a new lover and she's going to his apartment. Even
as she waits, she sees herself sitting on his bed
as he unfastens the buttons of her blouse.
He will cup her breasts in his hands. A sudden
breeze will invade the room, making the dust
motes dance and sparkle as if each bright
spot were a single sharp-eyed intelligence,
as if the vast legion of the dead had come
with their unbearable jumble of envy and regret
to watch the man as he drops his head,
presses his mouth to the erect nipple.

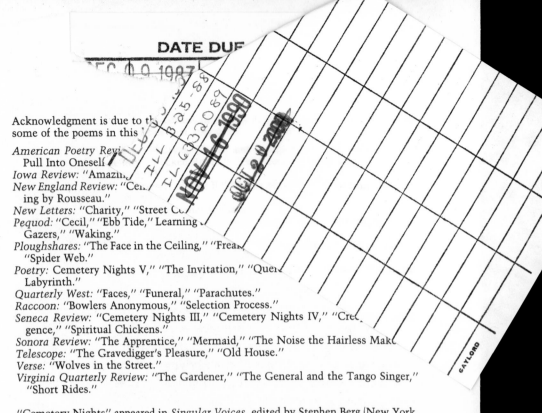

Acknowledgment is due to the ~~~~ some of the poems in this ~~~~

American Poetry Review: ~~~~
  Pull Into Oneself ~~~~
Iowa Review: "Amazing ~~~~
New England Review: "Ce~~~~
  ing by Rousseau."
New Letters: "Charity," "Street C~~~~
Pequod: "Cecil," "Ebb Tide," Learning ~~~~
  Gazers," "Waking."
Ploughshares: "The Face in the Ceiling," "Frea~~~~
  "Spider Web."
Poetry: Cemetery Nights V," "The Invitation," "Que~~~~
  Labyrinth."
Quarterly West: "Faces," "Funeral," "Parachutes."
Raccoon: "Bowlers Anonymous," "Selection Process."
Seneca Review: "Cemetery Nights III," "Cemetery Nights IV," "Cre~~~~
  gence," "Spiritual Chickens."
Sonora Review: "The Apprentice," "Mermaid," "The Noise the Hairless Mak~~~~
Telescope: "The Gravedigger's Pleasure," "Old House."
Verse: "Wolves in the Street."
Virginia Quarterly Review: "The Gardener," "The General and the Tango Singer,"
  "Short Rides."

"Cemetery Nights" appeared in *Singular Voices*, edited by Stephen Berg (New York,
  1985), and in *New American Poets of the 80s*, edited by Jack Myers and Roger
  Weingarten (Green Harbor, 1985).

"The Face in the Ceiling," "How to Like It" and "Spider Web" also appeared in *The
  Bread Loaf Anthology of Contemporary Literature*, edited by Robert Pack, Sydney
  Lea, and Jay Parini (Hanover and London, 1985).

Grateful thanks are also due to the Guggenheim Foundation and to the National
  Endowment for the Arts for fellowships, and to the Corporation of Yaddo, which
  granted me the time to work on some of these poems.

Grateful acknowledgment is made for permission to reprint the following material:

Excerpt from "The Song of the Happy Shepherd" from *The Poems of W. B. Yeats*,
  edited by Richard J. Finneran (New York: Macmillan, 1983). By permission of
  A. P. Watt Ltd., on behalf of Michael B. Yeats and Macmillan London, Ltd.

Excerpt from "What a Day It Was" by David Byrne. © 1982 Index Music Inc. Reprinted
  with permission.